"We need to go into my room," Sage whispered against her ear. "It's right behind me."

A given, really, at this point. Yet Kasey moved only to bring them together in still another deep kiss. Sage's hands unfastening her bra felt wonderful, moving warmly over her back, sliding boldly around to cover her breasts. Her leg was lifted up and around Sage's thigh while Sage's lips traveled the curve of her throat to the base of her neck. The low moan she heard was her own, flowing free as her head tilted backward in a dizzy heat. "Let me take you the rest of the way," Sage whispered hot against Kasey's chest. "Let me taste you."

Visit

Bella Books

at

BellaBooks.com

or call our toll-free number

1-800-729-4992

Love in the
BALANCE

by

MARIANNE K. MARTIN

Bella
BOOKS

2001

Bella Books, Inc.
P.O. Box 10543
Tallahassee, FL 32302

First published 1998 by Naiad Press

Printed in the United States of America on acid-free paper
First Edition: December 2001
Second Printing: February 2004

Editor: Lila Empson
Cover designer: Bonnie Liss (Phoenix Graphics)

ISBN 1-931513-08-2

To Jo

for her courage and love

Acknowledgments

If in fact an aptitude for written expression is in the genes, then I must give credit and recognition to my grandmother, whom I barely knew. Margaret Nickerson Martin, poet and artist, explained it perfectly when she wrote:

> *Out of the evening dusk*
> *there drifts the poet's song,*
> *singing because he must . . .*
> *knowing the night is long.*

ONE

Precisely at two-fifteen there was a knock on the open door of Connie's office.

"Excuse me," came the voice from the doorway. "I didn't see a secretary. Are you Ms. Bradford?"

Connie Bradford responded absently, finishing the last column of numbers before looking up. When she did, her eyes lifted to a vision in pastel green waiting in her doorway, a woman plucked straight from the sands of a sun-drenched California beach.

"If you're Katrina Hollander, I am. But if you're a sales representative, I am the secretary." The smile that greeted

1

her, gleaming white against the golden tan face, was as warm and genuine as the handshake. "A new department title brings sales reps out of the woodwork," Connie offered with a polite smile. She motioned to the buttoned leather chair in front of her desk. "Have a seat, Ms. Hollander."

"Please, everyone calls me Kasey."

While her newest client eased gracefully into the chair before her, Connie mused at how far from her expectation this attractive blond in a linen suit was. "Can I get you a cup of coffee?"

"Ice water would be perfect."

Connie Bradford moved on steady heels from behind the large mahogany desk, aware that her client was now making observations of her new accountant. She offered the glass, as her own eyes slipped down the shapely legs draped with natural ease at the knee. Her resulting smile was a private response — a rebuttal to the ill-based, gender-biased logic of the man in her life. "A woman in the trades," predicted Greg Morse, "has gotta be a dyke." Yet she suspected that were he meeting Ms. Hollander right now, his eyes staring boldly down the blouseless vee of her jacket, his predictable little mind would be groping frantically for the first cliché of a come-on he could find. A sad testament to the origin of his theory.

"Not what you expected?"

Caught in her observation, Connie locked onto eyes as intensely blue as a clear summer sky.

"Me," Kasey explained. "I'm not what you expected."

Connie retreated to the high-back chair behind her desk. "Not exactly. How did you come to own a renovation company?"

Kasey looked as if she were studying Connie's model-worthy features and smiled. "Maybe the same way a woman like you became an accountant."

"A woman like me watched her father's company fail because he didn't get sound financial advice when he needed it." Continued eye contact challenged Connie's sharp, defensive edge. Her tone softened, but remained businesslike. "This department represents a personal goal, to be able to offer the vast professional services of a large firm to the small independent business–owner like yourself. We've succeeded in keeping the cost down and have tailored our services to fit the specific needs of a small company." Her voice now carried a distinctly more personal tone. "I'm sure you've worked hard to accomplish what you have in the past two years. I'd like to do all I can to ensure that your company will be flourishing five years from now."

"That's something we would both like. I have to admit, a business degree didn't do much to ensure it. Experience, I've found, is proving to be the better teacher."

"It looks to me," Connie motioned to the folder on her desk, "as though you've made wise decisions — undertaking projects a small company could finish on time, growing gradually, investing in good turnaround homes." She finally relaxed in her chair and offered a smile. "In fact, you're doing fine."

"Then why am I about to give you my hard-earned profits?"

"You tell me."

A gleam of a smile brightened Kasey's face. "Because I'm a mathematical moron."

Connie Bradford, eyes twinkling with amusement, laughed for the first time, the easy, light laugh usually reserved for longtime friends.

"I'm serious," Kasey said, eyes dancing along with her half-turned smile. "Just the thought of an audit sends me into numerical shock. If you can spare me from that, I won't begrudge one penny of your fee."

It seemed her client wasn't so much sarcastic as she was honest, an attribute to be admired. "I'll certainly do my best. First though, I'll need you to fill out the information on these forms. It will only take a few minutes." As she spoke, she deftly aligned the edges of the papers, slipping them neatly under the clip of the clipboard. "I realize your schedule is tight. If I find I need anything else we can take care of it by phone."

She opened the folder of another client, intending to work as she waited, but found her attention returning to the woman across the desk. The intrigue, no doubt, had everything to do with the apparent contradictions between this woman and her career. *A business inherited from a father? A husband? Would I have even thought twice about her sexuality, had Greg not made his observations?* Greg's outdated, illogical quandaries both irritated her and forced her to waste time and effort ridding her mind of them. Intuitively, her own client had to remind her — she herself was a woman working in a man's world. *Is it any wonder that I need to be free of such incongruities? Free of Greg, and free of a mistake of a relationship that should have been terminated long ago.*

Pen resting loosely between her gracefully extended fingers, Kasey read the forms intently. Light played in reflective green on a diamond nested in white gold on her left hand. Rings adorned the right hand as well, but that one on the left represented exactly the relationship that had thus far eluded Connie Bradford's own life. A successful bridging of the intimacy gap between a man and a woman. Lovers experiencing a yearning between kindred souls, friendship, satisfying sex. Greg Morse need never to have applied.

Connie's concentration flitted over the unconnecting statistics of another client, but quickly returned to Kasey Hollander. Although he would never admit he was wrong, Greg would have to admit she was beautiful. She had the look of a Greek goddess, with makeup that Mother Nature herself must have brushed across her cheeks and touched petal-pink upon her lips. She was a woman who seemingly has it all: knockout looks, the drive and intelligence to run

4

her own company, and a man special enough that she wants to spend the rest of her life with him. *Some dreams must come true.*

Kasey made a last check over the forms before standing to smooth green linen over her hip. "I think that's everything," she said, handing Connie the clipboard. "Am I in 'good hands,' as they say?"

Connie slipped her hand once again into the warm firm grip. "You just do what you do best, and I'll do the same." She accepted an appreciative smile and added, "As soon as the papers are ready to sign, I'll give you a call."

TWO

Her new client's schedule was even worse than her own schedule at the end of the month. Connie called for directions to the job site and decided to take the papers to her personally. She arrived in front of the ancient two-story house at about noon, expecting Kasey to be taking a lunch break. As she got out of the car a young man, dressed only in a pair of painter's pants, emerged to retrieve something from the truck in the driveway.

"Is Kasey around?" she called.

"Yeah, follow me," he said, watching as Connie closed the distance across the yard.

He was a handsome man, lean and road-construction brown, with sandy hair pulled off his shoulders with a thick rubber band. Paint-splattered pants hung magically at his hips. Instead of following him inside to find Kasey painting woodwork, they walked around to the side of the house where a scaffold, looking very much like an adult Erector set, stretched sixteen feet to the roofline.

It was one of those summer days where the humidity challenged the mercury for highest honors. Only thirty seconds out of the air-conditioning and Connie's slacks clung stubbornly to her thighs. She wondered how anyone could work in this all day.

"Hey, Kasey," he yelled, his face tilted to the sky.

"Hey, Troy," came a voice from atop the scaffold.

"Somebody here to see you," he yelled. Then with a smile he headed back to work.

Shading her eyes from the sun, Connie spotted a head of short golden hair appearing over the edge of the platform. "Hi. I thought you'd be taking a lunch break."

"It's easier to eat up here."

"Show me how to get up there, and I'll bring the papers up," Connie offered, wondering if that was really possible.

"How many scaffolds have you climbed lately?" Kasey asked from her perch.

"None."

"I'll be right down," she laughed. With the agility of a monkey, Kasey climbed over the side and down an extension ladder tied to the end of the scaffold.

This could not be the same woman who had sat in her office in a skirt and heels. Sun-kissed muscles, larger than she had ever seen on a woman, flexed and glistened noticeably in the sunlight as Kasey neared the ground. The outline of a sports bra was the last remaining dry spot left on the gray tank top. Faded cotton shorts were soaked dark red with perspiration.

"It must be ten degrees cooler down here," Kasey

remarked, reaching for a towel hanging near the bottom of the scaffold. She passed the towel swiftly over her face and neck and chest. "Would you have really tried to climb this?"

"I think so. I'm no sissy."

"Another one of your services?" Kasey smiled again. "You surprise me."

"And you amaze me," Connie returned. "You actually do this work yourself."

Kasey looked directly into her eyes. "My looks are deceptive."

"Yes, they are." She pulled her eyes from the deep blue magnetism. "Well, here are the forms. Just read them over and sign at the *X*'s."

Connie wondered anew about this interesting woman. She looked considerably younger than her thirty-five years. *Could the man in the painter's pants be her partner in business and love?*

"This is a tremendous relief for me," she said, signing the last form. "Do you have a few minutes? I'll take you through and show you what we're doing here if you'd like."

"I'd love to."

They wandered through the old house, Kasey explaining where they had changed things and what still needed to be done in each room. "We had to widen the stairway all the way up to meet the thirty-six-inch code and shore up sagging beams in the middle here. But she's worth it. This house is over a hundred years old and in good shape for such an old gal."

She watched the face of this woman, with all her knowledge of a man's world, and marveled. It was apparent how much she loved her work, restoring her grand old lady. And although Connie truly believed that a woman could do anything a man could do, it still surprised her that such a woman would look like Kasey Hollander.

As they neared an upstairs room, they could clearly hear the sound of a male voice happily singing along with a radio. If Troy felt any embarrassment at their presence, it wasn't at all noticeable. He hammed the last of the song over Kasey's extended fist and took a bow. Connie clapped. With a smile he pointed to Kasey. "There's the singer."

"Never mind," Kasey returned. "Come on, Connie. This guy's got to get back to work."

The last room they entered sported a beautifully retrofitted closet full of shelves, drawers, and pullouts. "Wow, this is great!" Connie exclaimed. "I've always wanted something like this in my closet. I've never taken the time to find the right prefab unit — you know, the ones they sell ready to put together. This is beautiful. What great ideas."

"Thanks. I'll build you one if you'd like. You'll just have to decide what fits your needs."

"With your schedule? When would you ever have time?"

"Sunday. Well, actually not this Sunday; I'll be at the cabin. Next Sunday I could."

"I don't even care how much you charge. It would be worth almost any amount to finally have that mess organized," offered Connie excitedly.

"Give me directions and I'll come by this week to get dimensions. Give me a call and let me know what night."

THREE

Infatuation was nothing new. Kasey Hollander had certainly been infatuated with a few women in her life, and more than a few had been infatuated with her. *No harm in that,* she thought, *as long as I can identify what it is. Just never mistake it for love,* she reminded herself, pulling up in front of the address Connie had given her. She was tired, bone weary actually. However long and hard she needed to work to meet a deadline or to stay on schedule, she would. So why was she here, making an impossible schedule all but inhuman? There was no other explanation for it. She was fascinated with this woman. And Kasey knew from experience, the best way to get over it was to get better acquainted. The result would be one of two things, a nonsexual friendship or no relationship at all. And that, she decided, would be fine. She was no longer a teenager. As enjoyable as the feelings of infatuation could be, they had no place in her life anymore. Getting down to reality as quickly as possible saved not only time but a lot of wasted emotion as well. *So, Ms. Bradford,* she mused with a knock on the door, *let's see what you're all about.*

Almost immediately she was face-to-face with the vision that had kept her company for the past twenty hours. This time though, she was dressed in perfect professional contradiction — shorts and an oversize T-shirt. *Amazing how quickly weariness disappears at the sight of a beautiful woman smiling at you.* "I'm sorry it's so late," Kasey apologized.

"No problem. I'm a night person. I'm on my second wind. I'll get you something to drink. Ice water? Or would you prefer something else?"

"Ice water, thanks." She sat on the couch and looked around at what she could see of the immaculate little ranch-style home. Not a speck of dust anywhere, everything in its place. Something like what her own house would look like if it wasn't a construction zone, she chuckled to herself.

"I should drink more water too, as hot as it's been," admitted Connie. "I do better on the days I run."

"Where do you run?"

"I circle the neighborhood and run down through Breckenridge Park and back, as long as I have daylight. Otherwise, I stay in the residential areas. A woman was raped in the park last year, so I'm more careful. Do you run?"

"I used to. It's been quite a while. Like a lot of things in my life, it's been replaced by a schedule that aches for breathing room."

"I am in dire want of a running partner. Maybe we could run together. What do you think?"

"I usually work past dark," returned Kasey, surprised at how quickly this woman was befriending her. Not that she was complaining, mind you.

"I have an idea," Connie suggested enthusiastically. "I'll change at work and drive over to your job site. We'll do a quick run, and then you could go back to work."

Kasey laughed, "You're a taskmaster."

"Come on, try it. Maybe the break would be good for you."

"Okay, okay. But let's wait a couple of weeks."

"I'll be there the Monday after next."

Kasey shook her head. She didn't even like to run. *So, why am I suddenly agreeing to do something I don't like, with someone I don't know?* In a matter of minutes she had gone from client to running partner. She looked at Connie's smile. *Hooked, that quickly, despite a distinct sense of straightness about the woman.* A sort of friendly naïveté that wasn't as concrete as pictures with a boyfriend or a man's name tossed casually into conversation, but it was there nonetheless. *No, this can only progress in one direction — physical attraction totally ignored.* She would share of herself only what was necessary. Not an easy friendship, but it still seemed reasonably feasible. "I think we'd better get that closet measured."

"Follow me."

Kasey picked up her notebook and followed Connie into the bedroom. The closet was empty, its contents piled neatly on the floor and bed. Kasey immediately went to work measuring and making notes. She made suggestions based on what would be stored there, and a detailed drawing soon made the ideas visible. "Will this handle it?"

"Perfectly. I can't wait to finally get this organized."

"I'll be here about eight o'clock Sunday morning. It'll take all day."

"That's fine. Do you want me to give you some money for materials now?"

"No. Wait until I see how much everything's going to be." She rested her hand on the guitar case leaning against the bed. "Do you play?"

"Not as often as I'd like."

"I've always wanted to learn. Would you play something for me?"

With a smile Connie reached for the case. "If you sing with me."

Kasey smiled and watched Connie settle on the edge of the bed. Long slender fingers with their painted nails deftly strummed warm-up chords as shiny dark hair fell softly forward across a porcelain-perfect cheek.

Sitting down next to her, Kasey listened to the soft, light voice accompany the skillful fingers through an unfamiliar song. Lovely sounds of perfect pitch enhanced an already beautiful vision and did nothing to diminish the infatuation she was feeling. She was busy taking in the details when the notes began to take on a familiar melody, "The First Time Ever I Saw Your Face." She'd performed it so many times that the words no longer required thought. Gently she added her stronger, richer voice, in a harmony that must have surprised Connie.

At the sound of Kasey's voice Connie looked up, fixing her own darker blue eyes on Kasey's. They finished the song together. "That was beautiful," she said, her eyes remaining on Kasey's.

"We do sound pretty good together."

"I mean you . . . your voice. Kasey, it's beautiful."

"Thank you, but I could listen to you play all night. Keep playing."

Connie finally smiled and let her fingers dance across the strings. They sang song after song. Their voices, sometimes blending, sometimes soloing, began nurturing the seed of a special bond. All the while they shared their talent, a

13

familiarity was developing between them. Beyond appreciation, it was a sense of inclusiveness, of allowing another to feel how special something is to you. For Kasey, music was a communication deeper and more honest than speech. Her voice in song offered truths of Kasey Hollander unrevealed otherwise. A safe venue, for it would take another as sensitive as herself to hear its message. And it had been far too long in silence.

Just singing again made her feel so good, like the exhilaration of a good workout, only better. Its expression cleansed her soul, and Kasey had needed this cleansing for a long time. Connie would probably never know how grateful she was to her for playing tonight, and it was probably just as well.

Glancing at her watch, she suddenly realized how long they had been singing. "God, Connie! You're not going to believe what time it is."

Connie collapsed backward on the bed, her head coming to rest on the pile of clothes behind her. "I don't even want to know."

"Well, don't be shocked when there's a knock at your door shortly and some guy in tights is standing there with a glass slipper in his hand."

With an easy laugh she replied, "Ah, yes. That would be my prince coming to take me off to never-never land. Oh, wait. I think that's the wrong fairy tale." She lifted her head from the gray suit on the top of the pile and propped herself up on her elbows. "Anyway, he probably refused to stop and ask for directions, so he'll never find the place."

Kasey laughed easily. "Thanks for playing, Connie. Tonight's been refreshing." *And much too comfortable. It is time to leave.*

"I haven't enjoyed an evening so much in quite some time. I thank you."

"You say that now, but I'll bet you'll be cussing me out in," she looked again at her watch, "about three hours."

Connie raised her eyebrows. "I'll probably be thinking about how hard it'll be for you to drag yourself up on that scaffold." She sat up, her face suddenly concerned. "Do you have to work up there tomorrow?"

"Today," Kasey corrected. "I sure do. But it's been worth it."

"Then please be careful? I don't want to lose a client as fast as I get one."

As they stood at the door, Kasey reminded her, "Don't forget, I'll be back a week from Sunday, about eight o'clock. That's in the morning," she smiled. "You going to be up? I know how you night people are on the weekends."

Connie laughed softly. "I'll be up."

FOUR

Troy looked at the boards and tools in the back of the truck with a puzzled look on his face. *Hmm, top quality, no knots. Wonder where these go,* he thought, entering the nearly finished house. "Hey, Kasey," he yelled into the middle of the house.

"Hey, Troy," came the answer from upstairs. "Take the tools by the door out to the truck, will you please?"

"You got it." Picking up the circular saw and portable worktable, he knew now the project was going somewhere else.

On his way up the stairs Troy heard the beautiful, sultry voice that he had missed for so long. He recognized the song and smiled as he hummed along. Kasey was hanging the closet door as she sang. He approached, holding an imaginary microphone and began singing along. With his arm around her they finished the song, singing into his fist. On the last note, Kasey reached over and ruffled his hair.

"I like to hear you sing," he said sincerely. "You're really good."

The slightest little grin turned the corners of her mouth. "Yeah, what do you know?"

In his most professional sounding voice he returned, "Actually, I'm a field representative from a major recording company. It just so happens that I'm searching for new talent in the area."

"Yeah, right, and I'm Whitney Houston in disguise," she laughed. "But you're a sweetheart. I bet if we weren't related I'd fall in love with you."

"Uh-huh, and all I'd have to do is grow boobs and have a little minor surgery," he replied, swishing his hips mockingly on his way out of the room.

Kasey laughed and watched the cousin she'd grown up with disappear around the corner.

"Hey," he said, popping his head back inside the door. "What's the stuff in the back of the truck for?"

"I'm building a closet organizer for our accountant tomorrow."

"Ah, Connie. Isn't that her name?"

"Remarkable memory."

"There's a woman who could talk me into shopping on Super Bowl Sunday," he said with a wink as he stood in the doorway.

She closed the closet door without looking at him. "Why don't you ask her out?"

"If I'm not mistaken, she's more your age," he grinned.

"And straight," she said seriously. "I'm not interested."

"Then why have you been so happy all week? And singing?"

Her tone was unmistakably cool. "She's nice to look at."

Realizing her change in mood, Troy left the room, shaking his head. He had touched a sore spot and was sorry.

FIVE

The clock read eight forty-five. Connie had already
removed everything from her closet, taken a shower, fixed
her hair, and made sure she had everything needed to cook
dinner later. For the next fifteen minutes she rushed around
the house, dusting, moving this, straightening that.
Normally by this time she would have assumed Kasey
wasn't coming and been justifiably irritated. But something
made her sure she was only very late, and somehow even
that didn't bother her. Kasey's own words came to mind,
"You going to be up?" They only made her smile.

Connie Bradford had never before found so many reasons

to call a client. Some were business related, and some, she rationalized, had to do with today's undertaking. She hadn't, however, hesitated to call at the slightest excuse. Interwoven throughout her workdays now was curiosity about Kasey Hollander, about her interests and tastes. She guessed at her goals and her fears and wondered if this was a woman who could provide the friendship absent in her life. Was she capable of the loyal companionship for which she herself seemed to be incessantly searching? Of the friendship that could provide a gentle understanding of her needs, as well as a wall of strength in the face of doubt? Of quiet evenings, shared interests, unshakable support, and all those things that had always been too much to expect from friendship, although she always had.

Intuitively, she had never expected so much from the men she dated. And neither her father, nor her brother, had shown such capabilities. It seemed only possible from another woman. She had found bits and pieces and interludes, some with her mother and some with her sister and her college friends. Yet the enduring whole of it had eluded her, and somehow, stubbornly, the hope of its possibility remained. Now for the first time in years she felt compelled to try again.

A sound from the front sent her to the window. Kasey was backing her truck into the driveway. "I'll help you carry things," she yelled halfway out the door.

"I'm sorry I'm so late. I turned off the alarm and went right back to sleep. I hardly ever do that."

Her sincerity quickly erased all temptation to rub in her earlier comment. "No big deal. I got a lot done this morning. Where do you want everything?"

All morning and into the late afternoon, Kasey worked diligently on her creation. Steadily the empty closet became transformed into a functional, efficient space. Connie, too, worked consistently, organizing and sorting the contents. Anything that didn't fit, or that she hadn't worn in over a year, went into giveaway bags. It was exciting to finally be able to organize one of the most commonly used areas of her house. She must have thanked Kasey twenty times.

"Ooh, nice dress," Kasey remarked, entering the bedroom as Connie smoothed the peach dress out on the bed.

"Thanks. I think this is the one I'm going to wear to the open house next month."

"Is that the open house I received an invitation to yesterday?"

"The very one. The company's honoring my new department. You're coming, aren't you?"

"I wouldn't miss it. Besides, it gives me a good excuse to buy a new outfit. I'm going to have to make time to go shopping pretty quick," she replied, disappearing into the closet.

"You want company? I love to shop."

"Sure, that'd be fun."

She stuck her head into the closet. "You gonna be ready to eat pretty soon?"

"About an hour ought to do it. I'll finish this up and clean up my mess out back."

"Okay, I'm putting dinner on now. It should be ready when you are."

"No, you don't have to do that, Connie. We could just pick up some sandwiches or something."

"It's no problem. I love to cook, and I rarely have this opportunity. I don't want to hear any argument." She looked into Kasey's uplifted face. "Do you like Cornish hen and mashed potatoes?"

"I could be partial to almost anything home cooked. It's something I don't do well myself."

"Okay, it's settled. I'll be in the kitchen."

She stood at the kitchen window, spellbound by the beauty of Kasey's movements. Fluid and strong, the muscles of her arms and legs rolled and flexed, while the lines that defined them alternately appeared and disappeared. Nothing she did was gauche or abrupt. Even the most mundane movements had a certain grace about them. Connie had always appreciated the beauty of the female body, especially when it was so close to perfection. She found an enchantment to the bend of Kasey's body and the taper of her back as it slipped smoothly into the faded waistband. Watching her was an accepted pleasure. But it was one of those pleasures in life that she had always kept to herself.

The allure of Kasey Hollander though, she quickly reminded herself, was not merely physical. There was definite appeal in her independence, in her disregard for traditional boundaries, and in her love of music. *Exactly the kind of person I need — someone who asks the same things of life, who would respect me for my abilities and lend support for my goals, someone to whom I can offer the same in return.*

Before she realized it, Kasey was picking up her tools and bagging up scrap pieces of wood. How long she'd stood watching her, Connie couldn't say. Dinner had apparently fixed itself. Suddenly Kasey looked up and noticed her watching. Connie felt a rare twinge of . . . certainly not embarrassment. It was a rare occasion that Connie Bradford found anything embarrassing. "Dinner will be ready shortly," she said quickly. "I hope you're hungry."

"Starved. Let me get washed up," she replied, brushing past Connie. "I probably smell like a goat."

"No. You don't." *Greg after a workout — now that would challenge a few dirty goat butts.*

* * * * *

22

Kasey emerged from the bathroom just as the phone rang.

"Hi. Just getting ready to eat." Connie rolled her eyes and motioned for Kasey to sit. "No. I told you I was busy today. Yeah, well . . . it can't be helped . . . getting my closet done. Don't be stupid, Greg. I hate it when you do that . . . no. I don't know. I'll call you." Connie hung up the phone with a look of disgust on her face. "Why are guys so obnoxious?" *And controlling, self-indulgent, and egotistical. But* obnoxious *will do for now.*

Kasey responded with only a sly grin, and Connie continued. "When are you getting married?"

"I'm not."

"I assumed from the ring . . ."

"My mother's."

"Are you involved in a relationship?"

Kasey's brow furrowed in the place just above her nose, but there was a remnant of a grin on her lips. "Not right now."

"I'm sorry. When I'm not careful I start sounding like a female Jack Webb. 'Just the facts, ma'am,' " she smiled. "I apologize if I'm being precipitous. It's just that some good ol' unmarried advice would be much appreciated. I already know what my married friends would tell me."

"And what would that be?"

"What a great guy Greg is. They've told me how foolish I'd be if I don't marry him . . . as if I'd forgotten their complaints of married life." She passed the potatoes across to Kasey. "They think I'm expecting to find the perfect relationship."

"Are you?"

"I'm not under that delusion. Maybe they're more willing to live with things that I'm not. Or maybe it's the misery-loves-company syndrome. Either way, I'm not getting the objectivity I need."

"I don't know if I'm a good one to give advice."

"Why do you say that?"

"I was in a relationship for over three years. It was very complicated and even kept me from starting my business. But as bad as it got, I knew I wasn't going to be the one to leave."

"He left you?"

Kasey took a bite of chicken and nodded.

For a moment she wished she hadn't asked. *Why would a talented, self-sufficient woman with looks like Kasey's hang on to a bad relationship? Whatever the reason, it was totally irrational.* "Was he jealous of you having a career?"

"No. It didn't look good for a woman to be doing this kind of work. This is excellent, Connie. Thanks for treating me to such a delicious dinner."

"I'm glad you like it," she said quickly, slightly irritated at the departure from purposeful conversation. She put it right back on track. "Why is it that we put up with that kind of thinking for so long? I've done the same thing with Greg. Being free of that kind of pressure must feel wonderful."

Kasey smiled curiously and took a sip of coffee. "Do you love him?"

Connie looked her directly in the eye. "I thought I did, once."

"Then what decision is there to make? Unless you still want the sex part of the relationship."

Exactly, Kasey. Exactly what's needed here — a straightforward, logical discussion of the situation. Precisely what a friend should do. "You make it sound so simple. No, for me sex is not a necessity, it's an option. One I don't want with Greg."

"It sounds like you've made your decision. I don't understand what the problem is."

"Getting him, and everyone else I guess, to accept that it's over."

"Have you told him you don't want to see him anymore?"

"Yes, rather bluntly. I thought I made it clear that I don't love him. Of course he's sure there's someone else."

Kasey began clearing the dishes from the table. "Probably easier on his ego."

"Mmm. He'd relish the chance to push his chest at some guy and challenge him to take me from him. Jealousy of someone having something he considered his is what he feels. Not love. He hasn't a clue of what love is." She drew dishwater as she spoke. "The problem is that if there is no one else he has no one to confront except himself."

"And you."

"Naturally. It's not his fault."

"Is he harassing you?" Kasey asked, pulling the dish towel off the handle of the stove.

"Harassment?" Her brow squeezed into a pensive frown. "He hasn't given up yet. I took my key off his key ring last week. I was afraid that if I asked him for it he'd make a copy first. He's dealing with his anger right now."

"Has he ever hit you?"

"No. He's looked like he wanted to a couple of times, but he threw something instead."

"I've learned never to trust that a man can control his anger."

The look in Kasey's eyes was all that was needed for Connie to know that the words were spoken from experience. "In all honesty, I've been the one guilty of inflicting most of the pain, emotional pain, that is. I've said things that I knew blew his ego right out of the water. But I didn't know how else to do it."

Kasey's tone was tempered, her gaze somewhat distant. "Then what is it you need from me?"

"A word of support from someone I hardly know. Seems a strange thing to need when you put it into words."

"Not really. Support is important. You get it wherever you can. You can't be responsible for making someone else happy; only yourself. And only you can know how to do that. That's a lesson I had to learn the hard way." The seriousness in her face softened into a gentle smile. "My objective viewpoint, for what it's worth."

"Most valuable. The only one I've gotten so far."

"Kasey, before I forget, give me your bill. I'll write you a check."

Kasey produced a piece of paper from her clipboard as they relaxed in the living room.

Connie looked it over quickly. "No wonder you need an accountant. It looks like you put the tax in the space intended for labor cost."

"No, that's what I meant to charge you. Don't forget, you fed me a wonderful dinner."

"No, Kasey. I'm not letting you work all day for ten dollars."

"Listen, don't argue with me. It wasn't hard to do, and I enjoy your company. Besides, I was hoping maybe you'd teach me to play the guitar."

"Are you sure that's a fair trade?"

"Yes, I'm sure," Kasey answered with a smile.

"All right, then we start right now," she said, marching into the bedroom. "Kasey?" she called from the other room.

"Yeah?"

"Have I told you how beautiful this closet is?"

Kasey laughed. "About a dozen times."

The sound of the doorbell was unexpected. "Kasey, would you answer it? I'll be right out."

A pseudointellect, handsome even without his three-piece, stood on the other side of the door. His eyes made a brazen assessment of Kasey from her head to her feet, before he rudely pushed past her. "Where's Connie?" he asked.

Before she could answer, Connie emerged from the bedroom with guitar and chord books in hand. "I'm busy, Greg. What are you doing here?"

"I'll be out of town all next week. I told you I wanted to see you before I left."

"Maybe I should get going," offered Kasey.

"Not unless you want to miss lesson one. It begins in ten minutes." The look on Connie's face was clear — *Don't you dare leave!*

"I'll just pick up some of my things then." She disappeared into the bedroom before she realized how it might look.

In direct spite of Greg's stereotypical view of women in the trades, Connie dragged him into the bedroom and introduced him. "As long as you're here, come and see the closet. Kasey did a beautiful job."

He surveyed the freshly painted creation with all its pullouts, shelves, and rods. Then he surveyed its creator as she gathered her tools from the floor. "That paint smell is awful potent."

"Keep the door closed and the window open and it should be fine tomorrow," Kasey explained. "Connie, have you seen my studfinder?"

"What does it look like?"

"At first glance I wouldn't think you'd need one." Greg offered a cocky grin while he made his assessment of Kasey's legs and backside as obvious as possible.

Kasey made no acknowledgment of the remark. "It's a little gray . . . never mind, here it is." She bent quickly and retrieved it from the floor by Greg's foot.

His arrogance continued. "That close to me, shouldn't it have been going off or something?"

Kasey turned and met his cockiness with an icy blue glare. "It must not have been turned on."

The comment stopped him midbreath. He could do nothing more than shoot silent poison darts at Kasey's head while she gathered the rest of her things.

Connie stifled a laugh, but couldn't keep from smiling. "I don't even mind leaving this mess until tomorrow night," she managed.

"You can't sleep here tonight. Get some things together and spend the night at my place," he directed.

Connie bristled past him. "I'm sleeping on my own couch, and you're going home."

They entered the living room where Greg tried once more. "I said I wanted to see you before I left."

"So, you saw me."

With one last dart, shot directly between Kasey's eyes, Greg conceded. Behind him the door slammed into its frame hard enough to shake the dust off everything stored in the attic. Kasey merely raised her eyebrows and smiled to herself, while Connie locked the door after him.

"I must say, Ms. Hollander, you do know how to handle your men. I thought I was going to lose it with the studfinder comeback."

"Your men. And you're not so bad yourself. 'So, you saw me.'" Kasey burst into laughter and collapsed onto the couch.

The sound was contagious, sending Connie into a fit of therapeutic laughter that pressed her back hard against the arm of the couch. It was a wonderful feeling. She wasn't upset or anxious or angry. Only relieved. And it felt good. Sometime during the lightness of the moment her legs found Kasey's lap, and with the laughter turning to giggles, Kasey's hand draped itself naturally over the silky smooth skin.

"Have I mentioned how obnoxious I think guys are?" Connie grinned.

"Once or twice."

28

Connie chuckled again and pulled her foot up in an attempt to tickle Kasey's side with her toes. "No you don't," Kasey said as she grabbed her foot. "I thought you were going to teach me to play the guitar."

"I am," Connie said, bolting upright and picking it up off the floor.

"You feel pretty good about things, don't you?"

"Like the first giddy steps of freedom after years in prison."

"That good, eh? Well, I'm really glad you're happy. Now show me how to play that thing."

Connie sat close behind Kasey's left shoulder, demonstrating the finger positions for the chords as Kasey strummed. As she leaned into Kasey's body to reach the neck of the guitar, the warm, flushed feeling creeping through her puzzled Connie. It had been a long time since she'd been nervous enough to perspire this badly. Her valedictorian speech, maybe. No, waiting with her sister Cathy for the results of her breast biopsy. Silly to feel that way now, she thought.

Kasey mimicked the chords. Connie repositioned her fingers when she forgot. She learned quickly and before long was able to go through the basic chords from A to G on her own. The first time she made it all the way through without a mistake she turned with a smile, almost bumping noses with Connie, and asked, "What d'ya think. Is there hope?"

Warm, spearmint breath accompanied deep blue reflections from Kasey's eyes and shot a sudden, sharp twinge right through the middle of Connie's chest. Her pulse quickened. The feeling, so unexpected, caught her off guard. She hesitated before answering softly. "I, uh . . . I think you're doing great." Connie watched the smile disappear from Kasey's face and considered that there may be something wrong.

"You' an excellent teacher," Kasey said, pulling her eyes away. "But I never seem to be able to get out of here at a decent hour." She stood, breaking their physical contact, and quickly picked up the things she'd placed by the door.

"Don't forget we're running tomorrow," reminded Connie.

"I thought maybe you'd forget. Not so, I see."

"Did you change your mind?" Connie's pulse continued its race despite her attempts to slow it with deep, slow breaths.

"I'm just kidding. What time does the torture begin?"

"About five forty-five?" smiled Connie.

"I'll be ready. I'll see you tomorrow."

SIX

The front door stood wide open, and Kasey's truck was in the drive. Connie checked her watch before walking in, then hesitated just inside the door and looked around. There was no sign of Kasey. She wondered if she should go farther, or call out her name. But two steps into the hallway and before she could decide, she was almost trampled by a short stocky woman coming heavily down the stairs and charging around the corner.

"Oops, I'm sorry," Connie apologized, suddenly staring into glaring eyes only inches from her own.

Void of a smile, the woman returned bluntly, "Something I can do for you?"

Connie's uneasiness increased as the woman boldly considered her spandex running shorts. "I was supposed to meet Kasey. We were going to run."

"I'd say she's a little busy for that right now," she spat.

"Could you tell her I'll wait outside for a little while?"

The woman foraged in a box and grabbed a tool. "Sure, I don't have anything better to do."

Connie headed quickly out the front door, wondering if it might be better just to leave and trying to remember the last time she had been treated so rudely. She hadn't expected anything like this, not from someone she didn't even know. And she didn't like being made to feel like an intruder when she wasn't. Unless Kasey had changed her mind.

She paced slowly between the porch and her car. Five minutes passed. Ten. She could manage only short periods on the step before returning to the car, each time tempted to get in and leave. Being this indecisive was unusual and annoying. She leaned against the sun-warmed fender, alternately bouncing her knees back and forth. She couldn't make herself leave.

Finally Kasey appeared in the doorway with the other woman. Connie could only make out part of the conversation.

The woman slammed her hand against the old wooden porch column. "Dammit Kasey! This is stupid, really stupid! You never seem to learn, do you?"

Kasey's explanation was calm and inaudible. She started across the yard, but turned once more toward the porch. "Troy's nailing up the drywall for you," she said. "I won't be gone long."

"As soon as I'm done muddin' I'm going home. I mean it, Kasey," the woman yelled to her back. "I'm not hangin' around waiting for you."

Kasey approached with long, deliberate strides and a stubborn stare that Connie couldn't break. "Kasey, if this isn't a good time, I'll go home and run. I didn't mean to make this a problem."

"It's not a problem. Did you stretch yet?"

Connie shook her head and automatically pulled her heel to her buttock to put her quadriceps on stretch.

"I'm sorry you had to wait. I'm more sorry you had to run into Sharon first."

"I got the distinct impression I shouldn't be here."

Kasey shook her head. "C'mon, let's get going." She reached over as the two began to jog and grasped Connie's forearm. "Take it easy on me now."

"Okay, cupcake. Instead of distance, we'll go as far as we can in fifteen minutes, then start back. How's that?"

"I hope you're good at rescue carries."

Their pace was a moderate jog. Kasey wisely asked the questions and Connie did most of the talking. Down through the rural neighborhood they jogged as kids played, dogs barked, and the working class came home. The smells of cooking dinners tantalized them as they passed. "Fried chicken," Connie guessed, passing the driveway of a little white house.

Kasey continued the game as they passed a house with a big smoking grill in the side yard. "Steak?"

"Mmm," murmured Connie, veering to the right and heading straight for the grill.

Kasey smiled, quickened her pace, and caught up. When she took her by the arm, Connie stretched it out teasingly. Kasey ended up holding her hand and pulling her toward the street as they laughed. "Maybe this isn't such a good place to run," teased Connie.

Kasey quickly released her hand. "Have you been keeping track of the time?"

Connie made a quick glance at her watch. "Yep, it's time to turn around."

"Uh-huh, I thought so. We went over fifteen minutes." She tried to look serious as she gave Connie a nudge with her shoulder.

"Okay, we'll jog ten more minutes and walk the rest of the way to cool down."

"Sure." She held out her hand. "The watch."

Connie removed the watch and handed it to her. "You're in charge, sarge."

It was a quieter return trip, with both women finding it more beneficial to breathe than to talk. For Connie running was therapy, bringing fresh oxygen to the blood and enriching the brain. Running was a stimulation that fought off depression and created the endorphin high that she had grown to rely upon. A healthy high. She was addicted to it and fast becoming addicted to another high — the one she got from Kasey Hollander. She was happy right now, truly happy. Greg was in Chicago, and her new friend was running beside her.

The fact that Kasey's schedule was so tight and that she had had to make some sort of sacrifice in order to run with her today held a lot of significance. She was here not because she craved the ache in her lungs from sucking insufficient air and not because of the health benefits from pushing leg muscles until they burned from exhaustion. She was here to fulfill a need they both obviously felt, that of friendship. And she was willing to make sacrifices for it. No one had been willing to do that for Connie since Susie Fisher had "borrowed" her mother's car to rescue her from a date with horny Howie Hamilton. It would have cost Susie a month's grounding if she'd been caught. The empty place she'd left had been there so long Connie'd forgotten about it.

She looked over at the woman running next to her. *How had she become so important so fast?* "How you doing?"

"Did you notice?" Kasey hesitated for a breath. "I pushed it five more minutes."

"Let's walk."

Kasey raised her arms and clasped her hands behind her neck. Perspiration pooled in the hollow of her throat and glistened with each deep breath.

"You really did well, Kasey."

"Thanks, but I wanna lie down in the worse way."

"Not yet. Blood'll accumulate in your heart. Keep it circulating."

They walked for the next few minutes, breathing deeply, until Kasey spotted a grassy area on the edge of a playground. She took one step into the grass, foundered onto her back, and folded her arms over her eyes.

"Okay," Connie conceded, settling beside her. "How long has it been since you've done this?"

"Too long. Three years."

"You do amaze me." She reached over and placed two fingers on Kasey's neck, causing her to jump about six inches off the ground.

The reaction startled Connie. She pulled her hand back quickly. "I didn't mean to scare you. I just wanted to check your pulse."

"Afraid I'm gonna die on ya?" Kasey offered with a sheepish grin. "Go ahead and check."

Connie placed two fingers on Kasey's neck and picked up her wrist so she could see the watch. "Pretty good recovery," she said, resisting the temptation to gently fluff the hairs, dark with perspiration, lying limply on Kasey's forehead. "Do you feel okay?"

"Uh-huh. I guess we'd better get back." With Sharon's threat fresh in her mind, Connie rose quickly and offered a hand up. Kasey took it, letting her pull her up while she exaggerated the weight. Connie offered a gentle laugh and squeezed her hand. "Thanks for running with me."

"I have to admit I almost enjoyed myself."

Just over an hour had passed since they'd left the

house, yet both the car and truck were still in the drive. "Is she still here?" asked Connie.

"Yeah, her bark is worse than her bite."

"I'll bet you ran with me instead of eating, didn't you?"

"I worked through while Sharon and Troy ate. I'll get something later."

"I'll go get you something so you won't have to waste any more time. Don't argue with me. I'll be back in a little while."

Kasey admired the svelte figure collapsing neatly into the driver's seat. There didn't seem to be much sense in objecting. "I'll be upstairs. Just come on up."

Upstairs, Kasey checked out the room they'd been working in all day. "Beautiful job, Sharon," she said, looking at the freshly mudded walls. "You are by far my top mudder." She shot a quick wink at Troy.

"I'm your only mudder, and don't you forget it," Sharon snapped, finishing a corner seam.

"No chance of that," Kasey replied, massaging the thick muscles of Sharon's shoulders. She had known Sharon for — she couldn't even remember how many years. And in spite of her gruff exterior and quick temper, she loved her. Getting upset would only compound the problem. Eventually, Sharon was going to have to get to know Connie. Besides, she was just a friend to do things with, things Sharon didn't like to do anyway. "Hey, why don't you call it quits for tonight. I'll finish nailing the drywall. Then tomorrow while you're mudding I'll help Dad with the wiring in the kitchen."

"Then that's it, except for painting, right?" asked Troy.

Kasey nodded. "We're right on schedule."

"Okay, I guess I will clean up and head for home," Sharon relented. She scraped the remaining drywall

36

compound into the bucket and closed the lid. Kasey gathered the tools and began cleaning them while Sharon washed up.

After a few awkward moments of silence Sharon abruptly looked up from the sink. "Jesus Christ, Kasey! What the hell are you doing?"

"Nothing, Sharon. I did nothing but go running."

"Remember who you're talking to here? You can lie and keep secrets from the rest of the world" — she swept her arm outward — "but not from me, Kasey." She tapped her fingers sharply against her thick chest. Her eyes bored seriously into Kasey's. "Not from me."

"She's straight, Sharon."

"Yeah, exactly. So was Cindy."

Kasey tilted her head back and looked at the ceiling. Sharon's repair job over the sink was perfect.

"Have you told her you're gay?"

Kasey's gaze returned, but she made no reply.

"You haven't, have you. Why not?"

Still no response.

"Tell her right now, Kasey. Tell her and let's get this thing over with, one way or the other."

"When I'm ready, Sharon. When I'm damn good and ready." She turned to walk away but changed her mind. "Why do you have to get so worked up over nothing?"

Sharon wadded the towel and threw it into the corner of the counter. Briskly she pushed past Kasey. "You know why," she muttered as she left.

SEVEN

Connie slipped into the front seat of the shiny green Taurus. "I was looking for the truck."

"Welcome to my bargain-on-wheels," Kasey smiled. "Two years old. I bought it from a retired teacher."

"These things really exist? I figured that was only a story that was supposed to raise a warning flag at the used-car lot."

"Oh, and I suppose you don't believe in Santa Claus or fairies, then," she smiled.

"That would definitely be pushing it."

"Fine. Then at least sit back and enjoy your ride in the Clit Car."

"The what?"

"Sharon Davis humor. She nicknamed it . . . Clitoris — CliTaurus."

Connie laughed, partly because it was funny, partly out of disbelief that Sharon Davis really *had* a sense of humor. "Then you'd better treat her gently," she said, passing her hand slowly over the dash.

"Always. Where are we going? There are sales at the mall."

"Onward to the sales. Let's find you a bargain on a new dress."

Like shoppers possessed, they forged from store to store, rummaging through the racks and trying on clothes. "Connie, I'm going to try these on," Kasey said, whisking past her aisle.

"Wait. I want to see them," she said, looking up to find Kasey already out of sight. Hurrying down the aisle with a couple more outfits, she was suddenly caught by an idea. There at the end of the rack was the sleaziest, skimpiest, most gaudy piece of apparel she had ever seen. The combination of gold lamé and black see-through material was bad enough. But the tight bodice barely had enough gold lamé to qualify as a triple-A trainer, and the skirt wouldn't cover the tiniest of buttocks. Connie grabbed her find and slipped it between the other outfits. She could barely keep from giggling aloud as she ran to the dressing rooms.

"Kasey, I have a few more dresses here." She handed her choices through the curtain.

"Thanks. I don't like the first one I picked out."

"Let me see it," Connie ordered. The curtain slid open and Connie surveyed the trim, flawless figure outlined in blue. "What's wrong with it?"

"These," she said, tugging at the short sleeves. "I'd have to find a jacket to go with it."

"Why?"

Kasey ducked quickly back into the cubicle. "I don't like my arms to show."

"Don't be silly, Kasey. Your arms are beautiful." *How could anyone think any differently?*

She could hear the hangers being moved around from hook to hook, but still no response indicating Kasey'd found her surprise. Another minute went by. Connie waited impatiently, smiling to herself.

"This one's much better." Suddenly the curtain flew open. "It's definitely me."

Connie was stunned. Her mouth dropped open while a rare flash of heat flushed her face and spread quickly over her body. The surprise had been so effectively reversed. Kasey stood shamelessly before her, hand on hip. Previously unexposed flesh, creamy white below the tan line, pushed imprudently against the futile confines of the gold lamé bodice. What kept it in place was a mystery.

Before Connie could recoup, Kasey seized the opportunity. With a perfect streetwalker gait she swished into the hallway, snapping her gum loudly, and headed toward the mirror. By now Connie was in hysterics, and heads started popping out of cubicles to see what was so funny. Kasey continued the charade, stopping on her way back to adjust the material barely covering her breasts. The laughter had spread down the hallway as women in various stages of dress emerged from their dressing rooms to join the fun. Connie was laughing so hard she had to lean against the wall with her legs crossed. Kasey walked up to within inches of her and spoke in cracking spearmint. "Con, I'm so glad you found this, it's perfect."

"Dammit, Kasey, you had to pull this when I have to go to the bathroom," she managed, before breaking into laughter again. "I'm gonna wet my pants."

Kasey disappeared behind the curtain, but the vision of her remained. Then without warning, as Connie leaned against the wall with a smile, the vision turned from an erotic paradox into one of heated sensuality. Soft flimsy material clung tightly over smooth firm flesh. Hardened nipples taunted their confinement beneath the shiny gold. A warm rush swept through Connie, undefinable and slightly uncomfortable. She likened it to the flush of embarrassment. Yet she didn't wish it away. She wished only to hang on to it long enough to dissect it, to actually tear it down to its roots, until she understood it. Which, of course, wasn't possible right here and now.

The laughter down the hall had died to giggles when Kasey, behind the curtain, suddenly burst into laughter.

That was all it took to start Connie all over again. "Kasey, stop it!" she pleaded. "I can't laugh anymore. My face hurts."

"I can't help it. You should have seen your face."

"I've got to make it to the bathroom," Connie said, trying to concentrate on control. "I'll meet you in the middle of the mall." She moved as quickly as she dared. "By the fountain."

Kasey laughed quietly to herself. She had successfully broken through that unshakable Connie Bradford control, interrupted that efficient flow of movement that was never out of sync and never without purpose, and untracked the carefully plotted thoughts always set toward a mission. And what she saw pleased her. *Surely enjoyment this natural and spontaneous is safe enough.*

EIGHT

The banquet room was beginning to fill with people —
company employees and their guests, and clients and their
guests. Connie seated her parents at the front table with
her boss, Jack, and his wife. The invitations read:

REFRESHMENTS AND HORS D'OEUVRES	7:00–8:00
DEDICATION OF SMALL BUSINESS DIVISION	8:15–8:45
ENTERTAINMENT AND DANCING	UNTIL MIDNIGHT

It was nearly seven-thirty. Still no Kasey. Connie greeted
and mingled and religiously checked the door. Having made
at least a brief stop at each table, she relented and returned

to the front. "Connie, did you see Greg come in?" asked her father. Turning, she spotted him talking with another couple from his computer company.

"There's room for him to sit here with us," her mother offered.

"No, Mom, I'm not seeing Greg anymore."

Dad would no doubt miss their friendly football wagers and their political camaraderie. Connie would not. "What happened?" he asked.

"Not now, John," her mother directed.

"I'll tell you about it later," Connie promised.

At the same time she was becoming increasingly irritated about his being there. All week she had assumed he wouldn't be back from the convention in time. She did not want to share this with him. Tonight was hers, to be shared with her parents and with Kasey. For once it would be nice to experience a man graciously bowing out of a situation, acknowledging that it's not possible to control someone else's feelings. Logic, though, spoke loudly against that happening. She hadn't met a man yet with the maturity to handle that kind of rejection, including her own father.

Looking over at him she wondered what had happened between her parents to make her mother leave his bed? What happened to the emotion that produced the courtship poems she had secretly read as a child? Where had the sexual excitement of their youth gone? Was it possible that her mother, like herself, found sex unfulfilling? Enduring only to have a family? Or, maybe she caught him with someone else. Whatever it was, he'd been on the hunt ever since Connie was in her teens. Rejection made him act like a teenage boy; embarrassing to everyone around him. She never understood why her mother had put up with it all these years.

The piano was being moved to the front of the room, prompting Connie to move her guitar from behind the table.

"You look great," came a deep male voice from behind her. She turned to find eyes the color of rich coffee taking in the silky peach material folded softly in a vee over her breasts. "In fact, you're stunning," he added, following the material to the wide-belted waist and its gentle fall over her slender hips.

"Tom," she greeted with a smile. "I was just about to look for you."

He was lean and tall, his severely dark hair slicked back to perfection. A man with the graciousness of a true gentleman and admirable musical talent. It was his composition for guitar and piano that they would perform together tonight. She accepted his compliments without reservation, for in the three years he had done business with her company he'd never given her reason not to.

"You're not nervous, are you?" he asked, arranging his music sheets.

"A little."

"Don't worry. You play beautifully. It's going to be fun." His smile was reassuring, but far too brief. "Connie, someone just came in that I haven't seen in a long time. I'll see you in a little bit. Don't be nervous now."

Watching him stride off in the direction of the entrance area, Connie caught sight of Kasey's slender figure in the formfitting cream and white dress. She was here. Connie's pulse quickened as she began making her way through the crowd.

"Kasey," Tom called.

She turned and smiled immediately. "It's been way too long," she said, stretching her arms up to his neck.

He hugged her so hard he picked her right up off the floor and whispered, "You are the most beautiful dyke I've ever seen."

44

She kissed the side of his face with a smile. "How's everything at home?" she asked, back on the floor again.

"Couldn't be better. And this is Troy, right?"

Troy returned a firm handshake. "How ya doin'?"

Connie witnessed the hug from Tom, masked her surprise, and made eye contact with Troy. "You're a handsome sight," she said to his wide, boyish smile.

He tugged at the tie matching Kasey's dress. "Yeah? For a grunt I clean up all right."

"Hey, I didn't realize you two knew each other," she said, turning her attention to Kasey and Tom.

"I've known Kasey for quite a few years now."

"Tom was the one who told me about your company's new services," explained Kasey.

Connie gave Kasey's hand a squeeze. "Then I have you to thank for meeting this lady."

A thumping from the microphone diverted their attention. "If everyone will get the last of their refreshments and be seated," someone announced, "we will be starting the dedication portion of our program in about five minutes."

Connie excused herself. "I'd better get back up front."

Connie listened anxiously as Jack dedicated her new department. She smiled at his humor and attempted to keep eye contact with Kasey at a minimum. If only Greg would offer the same courtesy. His stare was making her more irritated than nervous. Otherwise, everything was moving along almost too perfectly. With professional flair, Connie introduced her new clients. She saved Kasey's introduction until last; the only woman among them. She wondered how many people were surprised to see Kasey stand and not Troy. The thought made her smile that much longer.

"For those of you who do not know Tom," announced

Jack, "he is the owner of Steppens Music, the largest music store in the city and a client for the past three years. He has written and performed for the civic theater more times than you can count, so I'm sure you're going to enjoy what he has planned for you tonight."

Gratefully, Connie concentrated on the notes. Her focus rested comfortably on the feel of the strings as she tuned out everything except the marriage of sound between the two kinds of strings. Her fingers danced with precision the familiar moves that sent the notes flowing in perfect harmony. Then the notes of the piano strings quieted, leaving the strings of her guitar carrying the melody alone. So easy it was to lose herself in the beauty of sound. It wrapped itself around her, flowed through her. She rode the drama of its crescendo, drifted gently on its descent. And for a time there existed only the excitement of its drama. Music was the therapy for her mind that running was to her body. Her solo was flawless. A faint smile showed on her lips.

Troy, with his arm draped over the back of her chair, watched Kasey take in Connie's every expression, every move.

Aware of his stare, Kasey turned. "What?"

He shook his head with a sly grin. "Nothin'."

Kasey hit his leg. "I'm trying to learn to play," she said, redirecting her gaze to Connie.

"Yeah."

The piece was beautiful and at its end received tremendous applause. Connie, pleased and relieved, finally looked toward Kasey.

Bravo, she mouthed, her eyes fixed on Connie's.

The applause became unimportant. Kasey had liked it.

* * * * *

"Connie, your mother is pretty tired. I think we'll go on home," her father said as Connie returned her guitar behind the table.

She hugged her mother's drooping shoulders and kissed the soft pale cheek. "Are you okay, Mom?"

"I'm just too tired to stay the rest of the evening. Congratulations, honey. You played so beautifully. You enjoy the rest of the night. I'll call you tomorrow," she said as she gathered her things.

While she watched them make their way toward the door, Connie listened to the unfamiliar notes of Tom's next piece. "This song wasn't planned," he explained, "but there's someone here tonight who sang it in a production with me two years ago. Kasey, will you sing it with me again?"

Connie looked to see a surprised Kasey shaking her head no. But Tom continued playing. "This is an Anne Murray/Dave Loggins duet called 'Nobody Loves Me Like You Do.'" With his eyes on Kasey he began to sing.

Apparently not wanting to make any more of a fuss, Kasey stood. She smiled at the thank you Connie mouthed in her direction, walked around her table, and began, "Love is glowing in your eyes." The strength of her voice carried easily without the microphone. She continued toward the piano, her eyes fixed on Tom, and picked up Connie's microphone. Beside him now, she watched as Tom sang his part to her.

Kasey had taken her captive. Connie no longer had the power to pull her eyes away. She watched helplessly as love traveled the notes, fluent between the singers. Their eyes never left each other, sending and receiving the music's message. A seemingly private concert to which Connie had become an unwilling voyeur, caught in a mire of contradiction. *She can't be in love with him. I don't want her to be in love with him.* Her body shivered. Perspiration seeped from every pore. *Can he be the man who left her? What if she loses her strength and falls back into his charismatic web?*

Their voices, singing from their souls, sang the chorus in unison. There was so much emotion in Kasey's face. Connie shivered again.

Tom sang, "You touch my heart in places."

Kasey answered, "That I never even knew."

Throughout the second verse Connie's focus remained fixed on the woman whose voice caused her soul to quiver. And like a video camera, her mind recorded everything, from the way her dress hugged her chest and hips to her lips, glistening as she sang. Nothing was overlooked — the shapely legs, the graceful body language, even the gold chain shining boldly against her strong hand. Connie's relentless gaze followed the long white sleeve, covering what she knew was a beautifully muscled arm, to the broad shoulder. There the movement of a long gold earring caught her attention, dancing seductively with every move of Kasey's head. Kasey looked down into Tom's eyes as they finished together.

Transfixed beyond control, she watched Kasey once again close her eyes and listen to Tom skillfully touching the keys that put their song to rest. Then she leaned down, with no mercy for Connie's bewilderment, and sweetly kissed his lips. Applause once again filled the room as Kasey turned to return to her table. For one brief moment Connie stared into the blueness of Kasey's eyes, her heart pounding a marathon cadence. No smile was offered; none was received.

The mass of entangled emotion allowed Connie only one clear realization — she was confused. Not about her need for Kasey's friendship; that need was an old familiar one. Her confusion involved Kasey's sexuality and the feelings it generated in her. Greg's crude labeling of Kasey as a dyke had easily been dismissed, considered born of hurt and jealousy. Her sexuality was irrelevant to their friendship anyway. It was of no concern. *So, what's so suddenly important about a relationship with Tom? Is it any less threatening to our friendship if Kasey is gay? There is no foundation for this reasoning.* And no foundation for her nervousness. Connie, the consummate professional, sure and confident, was having a difficult time understanding how the presence of one woman could cause such physical reactions. Normally, logic and deduction would have effectively put things in order by now. But this place in which she found herself was foreign ground. Nothing was cooperatively falling in order.

Unaware of how long she had been thinking, Connie's attention was suddenly captured by a hand on her shoulder. Tom's handsome face gazed down at her. "May I have this dance?"

"You may."

She liked Tom. She didn't like feeling that he was somehow a threat. But there were questions needing answers, and Connie was none too shy to ask them, diplomatically of course, and strategically placed around mutual compliments. "You and Kasey sing beautifully together," she said tactfully. "The duet was a wonderful surprise."

"Kasey has a tremendous talent. She really should sing professionally. Actually she had started doing some civic theater musicals, and a few weddings with me before . . . I haven't seen her for two years."

"What would you have done if she hadn't got up tonight?"

"Finished the song myself. I was pretty sure I could get her up there, though."

She accepted his genuine smile as a perfect opportunity for the big question. "Did you two ever date?"

"No." His eyes found Kasey. "We're just good friends with a lot of respect for each other."

Connie breathed a wonderfully deep breath. "That's so unusual," she said, almost to herself. She looked for Kasey's table as they turned. *What would it matter anyway,* she thought.

Greg unpleasantly interrupted her relief when she returned to her table. Her reality check. It had only been a matter of time. "So, how was the convention?" she asked.

"Fine. Nothing spectacular. There's an interesting new software program out, though. Something you might be interested in," he offered.

"I should be looking for a new computer, I suppose. Mine's a dinosaur."

"C'mon, dance with me and we'll talk about it."

Connie consented, although she could tell he'd already had a lot to drink. If she could only keep him in a congenial mood maybe they could get through the rest of the evening without an incident. As they talked, she noticed Tom and Kasey dancing near the middle of the room. Tom smiled when he saw her watching.

"Tell me, Kase, where did all that emotion come from?" Tom asked.

"Nervous energy," Kasey answered innocently. "I haven't sung for so long."

"Uh-huh. You going to let me in on who you were singing to?" he prodded. "It certainly wasn't me."

"How do you know?"

Laughing, he answered, "I know you too well. Is it our mutual friend, Miss Connie?"

Her answer seemed almost too quick. "No."

"Too bad. She sure has a flame burning for you."

"Why do you say that?"

"She can't keep her eyes off you. Plus, she seemed kind of concerned about our relationship."

"She's just a friend," she said, avoiding his eyes.

"If you say so."

Greg tried once again to pull Connie against him. Again she pulled away, this time refusing to continue the dance. "That's enough, Greg," she said, pulling her hand from his.

"You never have told me what the problem is. Why can't we get back together?"

"What! That I don't love you isn't enough?!" She turned abruptly and returned to the table alone, wishing she could just keep on going. Greg angrily headed for the cash bar.

Having spent what she considered a respectable amount of time mingling, Connie searched the crowd for Kasey. She found her with Troy and Tom. "Kasey, I haven't had a chance to tell you how beautifully you sang tonight."

"Thank you. But I hadn't expected to be put on the spot like that." She slapped Tom playfully in the stomach.

He grabbed her hand, leaned down and kissed her. "You handled it like a pro. Listen, Connie, I've got to get going. Congratulations again. You deserve it," he winked. "And your performance was perfect."

With Tom barely out the door and not even a chance to begin a conversation, Connie noticed Greg coming toward them. "Uh-oh."

"Drunk?" Kasey asked.

"Absolutely."

He sauntered up to the three of them, pushed his way in close to Connie and looked her straight in the face. "I want to know what's wrong with you." He motioned with his thumb toward Kasey. "You couldn't keep your eyes off her all night. What's she gonna do for you? She got a goddamn dildo under that dress?"

Troy moved decisively forward. "Why don't you pretend to be a gentleman and apologize to the lady."

"Time to go, Troy," Kasey warned.

"Shut up, Greg!" Connie demanded. "You're drunk. Why don't you get out of here before you make any more of a fool out of yourself."

But Greg persisted, turning his attention to Troy. "And you. If you were more of a man maybe your woman here wouldn't have to be messin' with mine. If she's a dyke, what does that make you? A fucking faggot?"

Kasey grabbed for Troy's arm, but it was too late. His fist was already making contact with Greg's face. Greg hit the floor facedown with a heavy thud. By now the commotion had drawn a small crowd, and for a few seconds everyone seemed too stunned to do anything. The combination of alcohol and Troy's blow was evidently too much for Greg. He groaned but made no attempt to get up.

"I'm sorry, Connie."

"He got exactly what he asked for, Troy. I'm sorry he had to be such an ass." She looked around until she spotted Greg's coworker moving closer. "Brian, would you please take Greg home?"

"I'll help you get him in the car," Troy offered.

"No problem. Looks like Ethyl was a little too much for him tonight," he chuckled.

"Thanks," Connie said gratefully.

Kasey turned as the men half carried Greg out the door. "I'm sorry this happened, Connie. You should have been able to enjoy tonight. It was for you."

Her voice was tired. "I half expected something to happen. Guys don't handle no very well."

"I guess not." *What do you say to a straight woman who has just been accused of lusting after you?* "I suppose I'd better get going. Troy's probably waiting at the car."

Connie nodded. "I'm glad you were here tonight."

Kasey turned to leave.

"Kasey, thanks for singing. Are we going to run Monday?"

"Sure. I'm kind of getting used to it," she smiled. "I'll see you then."

NINE

So far the weekend had been miserable. A chilling spring rain had fallen constantly for two days, while threats of a thunderstorm loomed heavily from purple-gray clouds. Kasey shuddered, not so much from the dampness against her shoulders as from the thoughts that had tormented her since Friday night. She knew she had to tell Connie and soon, if for no other reason than to end her own misery. *Greg certainly had a way of making a point. Poor Connie. She hadn't deserved to hear it that way. No, whatever the consequences, I need to tell her now.* Slowly, Kasey pulled into the drive. There should have been a better way to

54

prepare Connie for the soul-stripping revelation that was about to be poured at her feet. She took a deep, damp breath and knocked at the door.

"Hope you weren't real busy."

"Nope, just getting clothes ready for the week. I'm glad you called. There's nothing wrong is there?"

"No, just something I've wanted to talk to you about for some time now. Something I've been putting off." She sat on the couch while Connie continued into the kitchen.

"I just made some excellent lemon tea," she called from the other room.

Kasey was busy trying, for the umpteenth time, to decide exactly how she should begin.

"Here, try this."

"Thanks. It smells great." Carefully sipping the hot brew, she decided diplomacy was a must. She'd go slowly. "Connie, I think we have the basis of a very good friendship, one I definitely don't want to lose," she started.

"There is something wrong." Connie's face instantly lost its easiness. She quickly took a seat next to Kasey.

"No, really there isn't," she inserted quickly. "At least, I hope you won't think so." She took a deep breath and prepared to continue, just as the phone rang. *Damn! Not now. Not . . . now.*

After hearing Connie's cheerful hello, Kasey watched the expression on Connie's face turn to a look of panic. Now there *was* something wrong. She waited.

"Is she okay?" Connie asked, and then, "Oh, God. What hospital? I'm on my way."

Wide, frightened eyes looked up into Kasey's as the phone came to rest. Kasey felt the fear, the pure panic, the match for her own eyes two years ago.

Connie blurted, "It's Mom." Her voice quivered. Tears formed quickly. "They don't think she's going to make it." With shaking hands she nervously grabbed her purse and tried to retrieve her keys from it.

Kasey bolted into action. "C'mon. I'm driving. What hospital?"

"Orchard Hill," Connie managed as they ran to Kasey's car.

All the horrible, fearful feelings of that time in her own life returned to flood Kasey's thoughts. The intensity wasn't the same, but it was painful nonetheless. And just as it had done then, a tremendous rush of adrenaline put her on automatic pilot. She drove with a single mission, with no regard for the speed limit.

Tears streamed down Connie's face; her chin quivered uncontrollably. "What if we don't make it in time?"

Kasey reached over, took her hand, and held it tightly. "We're going to make it. I know every back way there is to this hospital. You pray and I'll drive."

Connie was grasping Kasey's hand with both of hers now, as if she could tap into the strength of it. She began to pray silently while large droplets splashed over their hands.

With one hand skillfully on the wheel, Kasey maneuvered their way down the backstreets and through the stop signs, squealing around the corners. She fought back tears when visions of her own mother, near death, crowded into her consciousness. They were getting close, very close. She looked for the service alley. There, right where she remembered. They sped down the alley and through the employees' lot where Kasey brought the car to a screeching halt beside the emergency entrance.

"Go," she directed. "Just say her name, and they'll direct you. I'll catch up."

Connie raced through the entrance and blurted out her mother's name to the nurse at the first desk. She was directed quickly to the intensive care area. Her father, disheveled and unshaven, stopped his pacing at the sight of his daughter.

She ran to him. "Where is she?" she managed through her tears.

"The doctors are with her right now. I don't know anything yet," he said, obviously upset.

Connie looked in the direction he had motioned and started toward the door. "No, honey. You can't go in. We have to wait," he said, tears staining his cheeks.

"No," she cried out.

He took her arm and pulled her back into his embrace. The strong hold of the thick arms and the faint, familiar smell of his cologne were her only comfort. They held each other and cried, Connie sobbing quietly against his shoulder. They held on to each other for what seemed like an eternity, until Kasey came running down the hall. Connie released her father and embraced her. Kasey directed a questioning look at Mr. Bradford. From the motion he made with his shoulders and hands she gathered there was no word yet.

Then suddenly the door opened and a doctor emerged. "Are you Mr. Bradford?"

"Yes. Is she going to be all right?"

Speaking slowly and ever so precisely, the doctor answered, "We're trying to stabilize her. We're not sure at this point what exactly happened, but we suspect an acute heart attack or stroke. I have to be honest with you. Things do not look good right now. If there are other members of the family, it might be a good idea to get them down here," he paused, making eye contact with each of them. "I'm going to let you see her in just a minute."

Kasey knew from experience what he meant: Get them down here so they could be with her when she died. "Write down the numbers, and I'll call for you," she offered.

Mr. Bradford pulled a card from his wallet with names and numbers of family members and handed it to Kasey. She hurried down the hall to the lounge phone.

Fighting the quiver in her own voice, Kasey called each name on the card. The memory of the last time she sat here, trying unsuccessfully to speak even the simplest words, tightened her throat. Her eyes began to water. *The least I can do is spare Connie this pain.* She looked up Connie's boss's number and called him at home. He offered his sympathy and as much time as she needed. Kasey acknowledged his offer with the realization that there would be many more before this was over.

Hurrying back to an empty hall, she noticed the door to the room slightly ajar. They were with her. Kasey entered the room cautiously. Mr. Bradford was standing on the far side of the bed holding his wife's hand. Connie was leaning over the bed with her face next to her mother's. "Did you get hold of everyone?" he asked quietly.

Kasey nodded.

Connie kissed her mother's face. "I love you, Mom. You're the best mother anyone could have." Tears falling, she pulled the chair close to the bed and held her mother's hand. The tangled mass of the all too familiar tubes was now visible. Mrs. Bradford was obviously unconscious, her breathing extremely labored. The nurse hustled into the room. Connie relinquished her post. Taking Kasey's hand, she watched while the nurse carefully checked her mother's vital signs.

When she finished, the nurse said softly, "We have her on the monitor, but if you need me for anything, push this button." Connie nodded, reclaiming her post and her mother's hand. From the tone of the nurse's voice, Kasey knew she expected the worse.

Like a pack rat, she began gathering extra blankets, pillows, cups, Kleenex, and even toothbrushes from the nurse's station — preparation for what she knew might be a long night. But all her busyness only partially diluted the memory of her own mother's ordeal. Ahead was the hardest, the part she knew only too well — the waiting, the awful waiting. For her, it had been eight long weeks. She prayed Connie would not have to endure that.

The hours crept late into the night. There had been no change in Mrs. Bradford's condition. Kasey tried making Connie and her father comfortable with pillows and something to drink, then settled into a chair by the door. The rest of the night was difficult. Conversation was sporadic and only masked the stress in attempts to keep Connie from crying, attempts that were proving just as important for Kasey. Their attention was centered every fifteen minutes on the nurse as she checked vital signs, and Connie watched nervously each time. Mrs. Bradford's vital signs had been slowly, but steadily, declining. It was indeed a long night.

As the early morning light inched slowly across the bedsheet, quiet voices from the doorway broke the silence. Connie's sister and brother-in-law had arrived. Kasey excused herself and walked the hall.

She sat on the ledge of the big window at the end of the corridor and gazed out at the neighborhood houses, a picture she had committed to memory. Nothing had changed on the outside. She wondered, though, if there were fears and pain hidden inside them, too. It seemed somehow wrong that despite pain and sickness and death, that the sun still shone, children still played, and people went on as usual. The pain was evidently too small for the world to notice.

A hand on her shoulder interrupted her thoughts. She turned right into Connie's hug. "I haven't even thanked you. I don't know how I can," she said, releasing her.

"You don't have to. How's your mother?"

"No change."

"C'mon. While you're here we're going down to the cafeteria. You've got to eat something."

"I can't eat anything. My stomach's too upset."

"Trust me. You'll feel worse if you don't get something down. Tell them where you'll be, and they can page you if they need you," she directed, taking Connie's hand.

Kasey called Troy with an explanation and a work schedule. He and Sharon would be fine. That was one thing she didn't have to worry about. Then she became Connie's one constant, staying with her as friends and family came and went. And then another night. Despite all the tests and medical expertise, Mrs. Bradford's condition remained critical. Her signs continued to fluctuate up and down, and no one had any answers.

TEN

The morning nurse awakened Kasey as she brushed by. Through her blurry, morning eyes, Kasey saw Connie asleep, her head on the bed, her arm across her mother. "Well, we finally have a little bit of good news," the nurse said to Mr. Bradford as he stood. "She's at least stabilized. That's basis for hope."

Connie had awakened in time to hear the encouraging words. She kissed her mother and caressed the soft familiar face with gentle fingers. "That's it, Mom, keep on fighting. You're doin' good. You're doin' so good."

"You know, if she stays stable the rest of the day, you

61

folks should go home tonight and get a good night's sleep. You have to start thinking about keeping your own strength up," the nurse advised.

"You two go get some breakfast," Kasey directed. "I'll eat when you get back."

Connie slipped her arm around her father's waist. "She's going to be okay, Dad," she said, trying to smile. "I know she is."

Later in the day, Connie's brother arrived from out of state, and for the rest of the afternoon the whole family was together. They embraced Kasey's presence quite naturally, expressing their gratitude for her efforts and concern. The sweetness and warmth that Kasey liked so much in Connie were evident in the rest of her family as well.

Soon, faces solemn with guarded thought and concerns expressed in quiet whispers were transformed through the nurse's encouragement. "Talk normally and positively," she said. "Even when people are unconscious they often hear what's being said. You should talk to her, too, and tell her who's speaking. After they've come to, I've had patients tell me what they heard and even who was there. Tell her happy things; it will help you all."

So throughout the day, family members caught up on the activities in one another's lives, shared the antics of their children, and addressed their mother as a silent listener. The result was a marked improvement in everyone's mental state.

"Okay, Kasey. We haven't heard anything from you yet," Connie's brother said with a grin.

The earlier arrival of the Bradfords' pastor had brought

to mind the last joke her mother had told her. "Well, I just remembered a joke my mother told me, if that would be all right." There were no objections, so she began: "It was Sunday morning, and realizing that her son was still not up, the mother went to her son's room. 'If you don't get out of that bed right now you're going to be late for church,' she told him.

" 'Aw, Mom, I don't wanna go. I hate goin' there. Nobody there even likes me,' he said, pulling the covers over his head.

" 'You get outa that bed right now!' she repeated.

" 'Give me one good reason why I should go,' he said.

" 'I'll do better than that, I'll give you two,' she answered. 'Number one, you're forty-two years old . . . and two, you're the pastor!' "

The joke filled the little room with laughter. The pastor, flushed with amusement, nodded to Kasey in approval. Sharing the humor that had so tickled her mother was a much-needed connection with her soul. But it was a mixed blessing that left her sad. She missed how her mother would try unsuccessfully to repress her own laughter, her lips pursed tightly together, unable to finish the joke. Her family had always laughed as hard at her as they had at the punch line when she finally managed to say it. She wished she could hear her mother's voice once again. She closed her eyes just for a moment, and, magically, the memory of her mother's laughter pushed past the sadness and lifted up her heart.

"That's really cute. Do you think she'll mind if I use that at next Sunday's service?"

"I'm sure she'd be honored that you liked it that well."

She looked at Connie, hands joined with her sister and her unconscious mother, glimmers of restrained hope reflecting in her eyes, and realized that the emotional connection with this family, with Connie, was unavoidable. Her own history locked her into their fears and their hopes. At this point it would be difficult, if possible at all, to separate herself from the inevitable ebb and flow of emotion yet to come. There was really only one thing she could do now. She would insulate herself as well as she could and be there. Walking away was no longer an option.

ELEVEN

The next two and a half weeks proved to be the most difficult of Connie's thirty years. Things that had held no previous relevance in her life had taken on paramount importance. Things like low blood pressure; how low was dangerous? And urine output; too little could mean the kidneys shutting down, the beginning of the end. Signs she watched closely now, every day and every night. Her family offered all the help they could, but because she was the only single one, Connie, along with her father, spent the most hours there. Her brother had returned to his family eight hours away and called every night. He'd be back on the plane in a minute if his mother's condition worsened. Connie's sister and husband, two hours away, had returned to a seminormal schedule and visited only on the weekends. Kasey came up to the room every evening, but Connie made her keep as normal a routine as she could. Most visits now resulted in Kasey talking her into a walk, or eating with her. Strategy quite obvious and appreciated.

After the first week, Connie too had gone back to work. She alternated nights with her father, sleeping at the hospital. Yet she was still spending a lot of stressful hours in that room. Every day she told her mother how work had been, how her brother's and sister's families were, and read her everything she could get her hands on. But now toward the end of the third week, she could feel the stress beginning to take its toll. She was rundown and so very tired. It was getting more and more difficult to look good for work and concentrate on her job.

Reaching for a glass of water in the early morning light, Connie looked across at her mother as she always did. But this time something startled her. Her mother's eyes were open. Connie jumped up, and in her half-frightened, half-excited state checked her mother's breathing. Her chest rose slowly, steadily. "Mom, Mom, it's Connie. Oh, Mom," she said, kissing her mother's face and hugging her. When she realized there was no response, she looked again into her mother's eyes. Eyes, usually so quick and sure, now held the innocence of a frightened child. Tears came to Connie's eyes. She pressed the nurse's button.

Almost immediately, the daytime nurse hustled into the room. "Her eyes are open, but she doesn't answer me," Connie reported nervously.

A smile appeared on Sherry's face. She leaned down

66

close. "Mrs. Bradford. There you are. We've been waiting for you. How are you doing?" Mrs. Bradford's eyes focused slowly on Sherry's face. Her lips moved slowly, but there was no sound. Sherry put her ear close to her mouth and listened intently. "An angel? Honey, did you see an angel while you were asleep?" She listened again. "She sang to you?"

Connie grabbed Sherry's arm, terrified now that her mother's mind had been affected. "Is that the drugs?" She hoped to God that it was.

"No, I don't think so." Her tone was reassuring, although the message still frightened Connie. Sherry looked again at Mrs. Bradford. "It wasn't an angel you heard. It was your friend, Kasey. Do you remember her singing every day? You heard her, didn't you?" A faint smile formed slowly on Mrs. Bradford's lips.

"Kasey sang to her?"

"Every morning after you left for work. If your Dad was here, she'd send him down for breakfast."

Connie moved closer to her mother. The deep brown innocence gradually shifted to meet Connie's thankful eyes. Suddenly her mouth opened as if she wanted to say something, and tears welled in her mother's eyes. She recognized Connie and weakly tried to lift her arms. "I love you, Mom," Connie cried, kissing tears from her mother's face. "I love you."

Sherry released the blood pressure cuff. "Her blood pressure's coming up. That's a good sign. Now, she may go in and out some, but keep talking to her. Just don't ask her a lot of questions. She can't really answer you yet. I'm going to notify the doctor and give your Dad a call. I'll be back in a few minutes."

The relief was overwhelming. Connie took a deep, exceptionally light breath. She smiled through tear-blurred eyes while droplets dripped from the bridge of her nose. She stroked her mother's head. Nothing on earth could have made her feel any better at that moment than looking into her mother's beautiful eyes.

Close to her ear, her cheek pressed against her mother's soft skin, she whispered, "God knew how much we would miss you."

She settled on the edge of the bed and stroked her mother's forehead. The thought of Kasey sitting here, singing to her unconscious mother, was the most endearing thing she could imagine. In all her analysis of friendship, what it should be and how it traditionally fell short, she had never imagined anything so selfless. Even her most idealistic hopes had never envisioned what Kasey Hollander gave so willingly.

As if on cue, the low tones of Kasey's voice carried down the hallway. "Mom," Connie said softly. "Your angel's here. Kasey's here." The chocolate brown eyes slowly scanned the room.

As soon as she walked through the door, Kasey was greeted in a firm embrace. "Somebody wants to see you."

"So I've heard," she smiled. "Mrs. Bradford," she said with a careful hug. "I'm Kasey."

Her lips formed the words slowly, without a sound. "I know."

"She thought you were an angel singing to her," Connie explained. "And I believe she's right."

Kasey sat on the edge of the bed, taking Mrs. Bradford's hand in hers. "I've never been mistaken for an angel before. I hope you still think so, now that you're awake. How about a song before I go to work. See if you remember this one." With a voice as soothing as a soft summer breeze she sang the words to one of Mrs. Bradford's favorite songs, "His Eye Is on the Sparrow." The sounds floated around them on the freshness Kasey had brought to the room.

Watching her hold her mother's hand and sing so sweetly filled Connie with a joy she never knew existed. She realized, in that moment, how very much she loved this woman.

Kasey stood in the doorway, about to leave. "What are you doing tonight?" Connie asked.

"Nothing special. Why?"

"I could use a real dinner. I don't think I could eat one more hospital meal. Plus, I'd like to treat you, to at least start to thank you for all you've done." As she spoke, Connie warmly clutched Kasey's hand, a gesture that was becoming very comfortable.

"You don't have to do that. I would love to have dinner with you, though. What time are you picking me up?"

"Six-thirty. And wear your new dress."

TWELVE

"I apologize for making an absolute pig out of myself,"
Connie said, finishing her last bite of dessert. "Everything
tasted wonderful."

Kasey laughed gently at her friend. "You should enjoy it.
It's a celebration dinner for your mother's recovery. I know
how hard this has been on you. I lost my mom two years
ago. I would have given anything to celebrate her recovery."

"Kasey," she said softly. "Why didn't you tell me? I can't
imagine how hard this must have been for you."

"You had enough to deal with. You certainly didn't need
another negative thought."

She gazed in wonder at the woman across from her. *What must she have been feeling? Every day, all over again. The fear, the sadness. Enduring emotional discomfort I myself had only touched upon by comparison. For me.*

"Listen, you know what you should do?" Kasey pulled out a piece of paper and began writing directions. "I'll give you my key, and you spend the weekend at my cabin. You could see your mom Friday before you leave and again Sunday night when you get back. You could even call and check on her Saturday. It's so peaceful and quiet there. You could get some much needed rest without one bit of stress." Looking up from her writing, she met Connie's questioning eyes.

"You can't come with me?"

"You're welcome to take anyone you'd like, or maybe you'd enjoy some time alone," Kasey said in a feeble attempt to avoid the real issue.

"Kasey, there's no one else I'd want to take, and I'm not spending a weekend at your cabin alone. That's ridiculous."

"Let's talk about it in the car," Kasey said, trying to take the check from Connie. Connie won the tussle with the bill held tightly in her hand. They left the restaurant in silence.

Once inside the car, Connie confronted her. "All right, are you going to tell me what's bothering you?"

"Yes, but let's wait 'til we get to my house." She remained in profile, avoiding Connie's eyes.

Connie shook her head and drove to Kasey's. Turning off the engine in the driveway, she turned to face Kasey and waited. *This is a very stubborn woman*, she thought, watching the beautiful profile.

Kasey finally turned and looked directly into Connie's eyes, melting away all the frustration. "Connie, your friendship means a lot to me. You've made me start enjoying life again. Even Sharon couldn't do that; she was too close to my situation. It made her almost too protective of me. Besides, Sharon doesn't like doing a lot of the things I do." She gave Connie not a moment to respond. This time she was going to get it all out. Finally, it was going to be over. "You've been able to see through eyes that recognize only me, and you've given me exactly what I need. That's why it's been so difficult for me to tell you what I have to. I don't want what I have to say to affect our friendship, and I know that there's no guarantee that it won't."

She took a breath, and it was all Connie needed. "Don't you know by now that you can tell me anything?"

"I hope so," Kasey said with an anxious breath, "because I'm gay. I'm a lesbian."

Connie never flinched, never moved her eyes from Kasey's, despite the little shock she felt in the middle of her chest. "That's it? That's what you've worried about all this time?" With a smile that seemed to envelop her entire being, Connie watched Kasey nod. "You could have made life a whole lot simpler for me, you know. Or was it fun to watch me floundering in indecision?"

Kasey's laugh released more tension than she had even known was there. She finally relaxed back into the seat. "Was I that confusing?"

"You're a chameleon. I'd think I had you figured out and the next time I saw you, you'd blow my mind."

"I've gone from an angel to a chameleon." Her smile was freer and easier than it had been in a very long time. "I really blew your mind?"

"More than once. Ms. Socially Conscious Connie wasn't as gay-savvy as she thought she was." She noted Kasey's amused grin. "A beautiful woman who wears linen suits and heels doesn't wear a tool belt and climb a scaffold for a living. And no self-respecting dyke, if you'll excuse my naïveté, would be caught dead for even ten minutes in —"

"Gold lamé."

"Yes!"

"I knew that blew your mind," she laughed. "I did it on purpose."

"Is that what you were doing when you sang with Tom?"

"What, trying to blow your mind?" She took her eyes from Connie's and shook her head. "No."

In light of their honesty, there was no hesitation for Connie to reveal even that which she herself didn't fully understand. "That was the strangest feeling I've ever had. The way you sang . . . I thought you were in love with him." Kasey's eyes finally met hers again. "And I didn't want you to be."

"I do love him dearly. But, I'm not in love with him."

"He's gay, isn't he?"

Kasey nodded, smiling, and noticed how cute Connie was when everything suddenly fell into place for her. The face of a little girl, filled with delight at having solved a tough math problem before anyone else could solve it — an analogy with no place in her own school days. For her, passing algebra had been a matter of laughing at her teacher's jokes until he came to sit on the edge of her desk and walk her through the day's problems.

"What's your relationship with Sharon?" Connie asked, jumping at her chance to clear the rest of the doubts that taunted her.

"Exactly what I told you. We've been good friends for many years. I haven't lied to you, Connie. I just haven't always told you the whole truth."

"You two have never been together?"

"No," she laughed. "We're polar opposites."

"And the person who left you was another woman. You just let me assume it was a man, right?"

"I didn't see any reason to correct you at the time."

"I'll bet I'm as relieved as you are that this is over." She took Kasey's hand again and held it warmly. "Thank you for trusting me with who you really are."

Kasey dropped her head against the headrest and sighed at the ceiling. "All this time relief was only a confession away."

"Does this mean we're going to the cabin this weekend?" Connie asked, more upbeat than she had sounded in weeks.

"We're going to the cabin. I'll call you tomorrow," Kasey promised, putting her hand up in a quick wave as she left the car.

THIRTEEN

It had never occurred to her that a three-hour ride in an automobile might be anything more than tolerable. Yet, the past three hours had proved to be thoroughly enjoyable. Filled with song and conversation and laughter, the time became irrelevant. Connie was aware only of how free and wonderful she felt.

"Well, this is it," Kasey said, stopping the car at the end of a long narrow drive that wound a full mile through the trees. In front of them stood a small, neat cottage nestled among the pines. A well-manicured little yard led down to a freshly painted dock that stretched out over the water. The sunset on the far shore cast a pink and purple reflection across the still, glassy surface.

"Oh, Kasey. Let's go down to the dock while it's so pretty."

They stood at the end of the dock, taking in nature's own light show and watching the colors get even more vibrant. Then, before Connie had noticed how quiet it was, a series of honking noises grew gradually louder overhead.

"The geese are coming in for the night," Kasey explained, as Connie searched the sky. Suddenly their traditional vee appeared from over the treetops behind them. Honking loudly, the geese swooped gracefully close to the water and glided effortlessly toward the south end of the lake. "There aren't any houses on that end, so they've made it their year-round home. They mate for life. See the space in the vee on the right side? One of them died or was killed. The remaining mate stays with the flock, but always flies next to an empty space. I felt awful the first time I noticed the space in our flock. C'mon, I have another place to show you before it gets too dark."

Connie followed her along a wooded path beside the lake and up a steep bank. Stepping carefully and ducking branches, they made their way to the top of a hill overlooking the lake. From the little clearing at the edge they could see the whole lake, its winding shoreline still draped in brilliant hue. "It's gorgeous," Connie said quietly.

They stood in silence, absorbing the beauty that surrounded them, enjoying the sights and sounds as Mother Nature began tucking away the day. "This is one of my favorite places."

"It's a very romantic place," Connie said softly. "I'll bet you've brought a few women up here."

There was a polite hesitation and no eye contact. The questions were to be expected. "Only one," she said, knowing she'd have to answer them sooner or later. "I really loved her."

"What happened?"

Kasey continued to look out over the lake as she spoke. "She was afraid of people knowing. She couldn't live like that. It was easier to marry a man she worked with."

Connie felt the weight of the silence but couldn't find words capable of consoling the sadness she saw in Kasey's eyes.

"We'd better start back," Kasey said, turning away from the lake. "Even I don't like going down this hill after dark."

They began their descent in silence. Partway down, thick patches of brown pine needles and small, partially exposed roots made it slippery under foot. "How you doin'?" Kasey asked.

"Fine. I'm no —"

"Uh-huh, you told me. Now take my hand," she directed. Just as Kasey reached out her hand, Connie's lead foot slipped off the edge of a root. Connie grabbed Kasey's hand to keep from falling.

"Okay?" Kasey asked with a smile.

"Yeah, thank you. This has nothing to do with being a sissy, does it?"

"Where should I put my things?"

"Put them in the bathroom, the door on your right. This couch pulls out into a bed. It gets pretty chilly up here at night. You can sleep here by the fire. I'll use the bedroom."

"You're not sleeping by the fire with me?" She watched Kasey silently placing wood in the fireplace. "I thought we could lie here and talk all night. Like you used to do with your best friend when you were little?"

"I thought you'd be so tired you'd want to get a good night's sleep."

"We can sleep in tomorrow, can't we?"

Kasey nodded.

"Then it's settled. You're sleeping out here."

Settling under the light blanket in front of the fire, Connie watched the dancing flames and waited for Kasey to join her. Mind and body were completely at ease for the first time in what seemed like an eon. The fragrance of burning cherry wood mingled with the slightly musty smell of old pine boards. The fire's warmth reached to the head of the couch and chased the night chill to the dark corners of the little cabin. Her eyes had just closed restfully, when suddenly something cool and soft hit her right in the face. Before she could respond, another pillow hit her midsection. She pushed the first one back hard at Kasey as she flopped onto the bed.

"All right, now you've had it." With surprising quickness, Connie shed the blanket, straddled a shocked Kasey and pinned her to the bed.

"Okay, smarty, now what?" Kasey laughed.

"You'll see." Connie deftly pinned one arm down with her knee, and with her hand now free started tickling Kasey's side.

"Oh, no," Kasey managed through her laughter. She struggled to free her arms. Weakened by the tickling, she mustered all the strength she had just to free one arm. She grabbed Connie's wrist and pushed up hard with her hips to throw her off balance. Then quickly taking advantage of the situation, Kasey raised her head and shoulders, pushed Connie backward, and rolled on top of her.

In an instant, Connie found herself lying chest to chest beneath Kasey, staring paralyzed into the intense blueness of her eyes. Their hearts beat against each other's in an excitement neither could conceal. Then came a look that electrified Connie's soul. She sucked in a breath and held it.

Shouldn't our lips meet now? Shouldn't I feel the warm fullness of her lips next and taste what must be the sweetest mouth? She was about to be kissed, she was sure of it. The flush from her face now consumed her body. Kasey wanted to kiss her. She could see it in her eyes. And Connie would welcome it, at least once, at least to see.

But just as quickly as it had happened, Kasey rose and rolled to her side of the bed. "Don't take that wrong," she said. "That wasn't a pass." *An indiscriminate, momentary lack of judgment, but not a pass.*

Throwing a pillow on top of her, Connie smiled shyly. "I took it as defeat."

Kasey returned her smile, busying herself with the arrangement of pillows and blankets.

Connie tried settling comfortably to face her but couldn't slow the rapid beating in her chest. "When did you know you were gay?"

"Wade right in, Connie."

"Inevitable question," Connie grinned.

"It doesn't matter whether I'm ready for this, does it?" Connie's grin only widened, and Kasey relented. "I guess I've known since junior high school."

"*How* did you know?" Connie added quickly.

"Probably a combination of things. I was a tomboy. I liked all the boy kinds of activities. And as I got older, I found I liked doing them more and more with girls. They never put me down or tried to make me feel inferior like a lot of the guys did."

"Something some of them never outgrow. Did you ever date guys?"

"Not for long. I hated them always trying to get a feel and turning everything into something sexual. I never wanted that from them."

"Did you ever have sex with a guy?"

Such relentless curiosity. Expected of course. But did it have to have such an annoyingly familiar pattern? She shook her head. "I could never get past the piranha kisses. They were disgusting," she said as Connie laughed. "What's so funny?"

"They are like piranha. It feels like they're trying to eat your lips." The vision made them both laugh. "What's —"

"Look, I know you have about a thousand questions. I expected it. But to be fair, let's make a deal. You have to answer every question I answer, only referring to guys when it's appropriate. Okay?"

"Deal," Connie agreed. "But this one I've sort of already answered. What's it like to kiss a woman?"

"Definitely different from guys. Erotic, sensual, emotional. I don't know how else to describe it. No whisker burns," Kasey laughed.

Connie crinkled her nose. "I hate that. You always have to make them shave." She hesitated as long as she could stand. "When did you first kiss a woman?"

"A classic lesbian experience. My best friend in high school was telling me about problems she was having at home. I put my arms around her to comfort her. I held her for a while. Then she looked right into my eyes and didn't say anything. Somehow I got up the nerve to kiss her, and she kissed me back. I thought I was in heaven. I kissed her the way I had always wanted to be kissed, and she kissed me back the same way. It was the first time I had ever been sexually aroused."

"What happened from there?"

Oh, no, you don't. You're not getting the juicy just yet, Ms. Connie. "We spent a lot of time together and made out a lot. She always said she wished guys would kiss like that. But I had no clue what to do from there, and I guess she didn't either. So that was as far as it went. She moved the following summer," she said, turning on her side. "Your turn."

Connie smiled. "Mine's really nothing. It was Jimmy Wheeler in the sixth grade. He was real popular, and it made me feel important for about two weeks. Then he started liking some other girl. I learned real quickly that relying on some guy for a sense of worthiness was a big mistake. They called me 'The Freeze' in high school. I was no doubt the cause of many a lost bet."

"I know the big one's coming, so I'm going to beat you to it," Kasey said. "What was it like the first time you had sex?"

"Ooh. It's definitely tougher on this side of the questions." She lay back and turned her eyes to the ceiling. "That didn't happen until my sophomore year in college. I'd been dating this guy for about three months. He was getting pretty frustrated with me. I guess I just got tired of making excuses and dealing with pressures from friends." Her eyes came back to Kasey's. "I gave in one night." She noticed Kasey's gaze move from her eyes to her lips. "We were on the couch in my apartment. He was shocked when I stopped fighting him. He even asked if I was sure. I wasn't, but I had decided to get it over with. I was very embarrassed. I made him wear a condom, and I didn't want to look at him." She didn't want to look at Kasey right now, either. "But I forced myself. The only foreplay was the little bit of necking we did before I gave in. I wasn't very lubricated, and it was very painful. But once he started there was no stopping him. After he left I just lay there and cried. I could hardly walk the next morning."

"God, Connie. I take it you didn't run right back for more."

"No, that cured me for a long time. Your turn."

"Mine wasn't terrific either, but at least it wasn't as bad as that. I was a freshman in college, and some friends and I wanted to learn to play tennis. We signed up for a class from the recreation department since it was cheaper than taking a class at the university." She wanted to smile at the red flush on Connie's face, but resisted. "Our instructor was a woman in her late twenties. She was athletic, very cute, and it didn't take me long to realize I was interested in more than her tennis skills. She had a bubbly, outgoing personality and teased me a lot. We started spending time together after class, and I knew she was interested in me, too. One day we went to get something to eat and ended up talking in her car until after dark. I knew something was going to happen by the way she was looking at me." Connie was watching her intently.

"She said 'come here,' and I did. We started kissing each other. Then she began kissing my neck and caressing my breasts, and I knew we were going to make love." She caught Connie's eyes slip quickly to her breasts, outlined in only a T-shirt, then quickly back up. "She drove us to a motel. I was so nervous that I wouldn't even take my underwear off. When she asked me if I'd ever been with a woman, I lied. She must have suspected, though. I'm sure she did all the right things, but I was so nervous I couldn't enjoy anything. I know she was frustrated with me. It must have been obvious I didn't know what I was doing. It wasn't until a week later when we ended up in another motel that I understood what an orgasm is."

Connie stared into Kasey's blue eyes for a few seconds, not knowing how to word the next question. Realizing her hesitation, Kasey said, "What are you worried about? It couldn't be any more intimate than what we've already talked about."

"I was wondering. When you're making love to a woman, can you stop if she lets you know she doesn't like something?"

The question, with all its innocence, made her smile. "Of course. Connie, I don't think of it as making love *to* a woman, I make love *with* her. The whole idea is to give each other pleasure."

"That's so different from what I've experienced. It's one reason I broke up with Greg. He was a terrible lover. I don't qualify as an expert. I've only been with three men, but none of them cared if they satisfied me. I felt like I was only there for their pleasure." Her embarrassment was easing somewhat. Speaking honestly, without fear of judgment, was an adventure in freedom. "Greg was always trying to get me to do things sexually that I didn't want to do. Just the thought of doing oral sex on him nauseated me. He wanted to have anal intercourse, too. There was no way I would ever give in to that." She grimaced at the thought.

"Selfish sex. And dangerous."

"Actually, I am very tired of dealing with sex at all. But I think I'm even more tired of their attitude. I see how my friends' husbands act. They don't see any reason to change. They'll be that way forever. The women either put up with it or eventually walk out and hope for something better. I can't see it." She paused for a second. "Listen to me," she smiled. "*I* sound like the lesbian here."

Kasey returned the smile. "No, you sound like a woman who is aware of what she likes and dislikes. A lesbian is a woman who has fallen in love with another woman."

"Is it really that simple?"

"If you can strip away the pressures of society and be true to your own feelings. That's essential whether you're gay or straight." Her advice reflected firsthand knowledge.

Connie thought about Kasey's words silently for a few minutes. Kasey rearranged her pillow into the hugging position and closed her eyes. "You're tired, aren't you?" asked Connie.

Her eyes remained closed. "Uh-huh."

"Thank you for talking with me," Connie said softly.

"Sleep well."

FOURTEEN

For hours Connie dozed on and off in a light sleep. When she was awake she watched the dying embers of the fire and thought about their earlier discussion. She could remember it word for word. The sun had been up for some time now, peering in through high little windows on either side of the fireplace. Connie settled back on the pillow and watched Kasey as she slept. With all the questions that had been answered she wondered how her mind could still be troubled, but it was. Finally, she figured it out.

Kasey stirred and opened her eyes. "Did you sleep at all?" she asked, looking at Connie between blinks.

"A little. I have to ask you something."

Kasey closed her eyes and smiled.

"Kasey, what is going to happen to our friendship when you start dating someone?"

Kasey opened her eyes to a very worried look on Connie's face. Rolling over on her back, she pushed the pillow under her head. "She'll just have to accept our friendship."

"You're not being realistic. We wouldn't be able to do much together anymore. There'd be too much jealousy."

"I know it probably wouldn't happen overnight; but given time, she'd learn to trust me and accept you."

"Like Sharon?" A little dose of reality, heavy on the sarcasm.

"We haven't given her enough time. Let me ask *you* a question." Kasey paused long enough to sit up. "What's going to happen when your next boyfriend finds out you're hanging around with a lesbian?"

"Maybe I don't want another boyfriend. Besides he'd probably just hit on you."

"What do you want, a girlfriend?" she teased with a raise of her eyebrows.

"Maybe." Connie lay back and looked at the ceiling. "Or maybe I'm asexual. I'll just have friendships from now on, instead of relationships, and leave sex out of it."

"Yeah?" The two women looked at each other. "Well maybe I will, too." She picked up the pillow and pushed it at Connie's smiling face. "I get the bathroom first today."

That morning they shared song and Kasey's improving guitar skills. Connie called the hospital, which eased her restlessness considerably and freed her to enjoy a walk along the lake. The afternoon sun warmed the day quickly, nudging them into bathing suits and the cool water of the lake.

"I'll race you," Kasey said, taking a head start. She beat her of course, and bent over to put her things down on the end of the dock.

"You cheat," laughed Connie. Before Kasey could even laugh Connie gave her a push, and Kasey was on her way headfirst into the lake. *You deserve that, Ms. Hollander. You can't beat me running fairly.* The glare of the sun on the water prevented her from seeing Kasey come up. She was sure she had; she just couldn't see her. "Where are you, Kasey?" There was no sound. "Kasey, are you all right?" Still nothing. "Kasey?" she called frantically.

She was at the edge of the dock prepared to go in after her, when suddenly a hand grabbed her ankle and she too tumbled into the water. When she came up, Kasey was laughing a few feet away. "How's the water?"

"You scared the hell out of me," Connie shouted at her.

"You started it," she laughed back.

"Don't ever do that again. I thought you were really hurt."

"Okay, okay. I'm sorry."

She slapped water angrily at her. "I mean it, Kasey."

"I *am* sorry, Connie. I didn't mean to scare you — not that badly anyway." She tilted her head and looked up into Connie's scowling face. She raised her eyebrows and gave her a little smile.

Connie splashed her again, but this time with a relenting smile.

"Okay, c'mon, grab your things," Kasey directed. "Hold them up like this and we'll swim out to the raft."

With one hand holding their rolled towels up out of the water they arrived at the raft and climbed out of the water.

They spread their towels on the warm, weathered wood and relaxed in the sun.

"Kasey, this is wonderful," Connie remarked, looking out at the view of the shoreline from her new vantage point.

"Another favorite spot."

Connie rested back on her elbows and closed her eyes. The warmth of the sun washed the goose bumps raised by the wind smooth again. She couldn't see Kasey's eyes making their own sweep over her body, lingering over the gentle curve of her throat as it met with the sharp angle of her shoulders, and stopping pleasurably on the firm full breasts. The choice of a two-piece suit was both wonderful and cruel. It presented a show of beauty as tempting as it was enjoyable. Unaware of her audience, Connie readjusted her hips. Kasey's eyes dared to continue over the graceful lines worthy of a dancer, assessing proportions exquisite enough for the camera. Kasey couldn't decide if the temptation was meant as a purposeful challenge, or was merely an example of complete naïveté. *Sleeping in the same bed — the wrestling match. What was I thinking? More importantly, why did it matter?* She pulled her eyes away and concentrated on applying sunscreen.

As she finished applying it to her face and chest, Connie sat up and took the tube from her. "How do you tan and keep such beautiful skin?" She began smoothing the cool lotion over Kasey's back.

"I don't work, or play, without this stuff. You'd better get some on before you burn."

"Yes, ma'am," Connie smiled. With long graceful fingers she smoothed the lotion into the creamy skin while Kasey leaned back and watched. When she had covered all she could reach she handed the tube to Kasey and turned onto her stomach. "Will you get my back?" she asked, unhooking her top.

Oh, no problem. I can lay my hands over the nearly

naked body of what I am sure now is a temptress. I can fight the thoughts that are making me warm, the ones that are causing me to dream again and teasing my still bruised heart. I can — I will. I will go on and bolster the resistance past this delicate balance, because really there is no other choice. Kasey warmed the lotion between her palms. Then, instead of merely applying it, she began massaging it into Connie's back. Gently but firmly she manipulated every inch of the creamy skin, from her neck to the top of her bikini bottoms.

"That feels wonderful," Connie said softly. Kasey made another pass over her back using larger movements with the whole of her hand. "Mmm, you could do that all day," Connie said with her eyes still closed.

With a gentle caress down her back, Kasey stopped. "No . . . I couldn't." *Well, if what she wanted was a reaction, then she had given it to her, plain and simple.* Kasey lay back on her stomach and turned to face the lake. She wondered if Connie knew how close to kissing her she had come last night.

"What was her name?"

"Cindy," Kasey answered without turning her head.

"Do you want to tell me about her?"

"Not really."

"Will you?"

Kasey turned onto her back. Shading her eyes from the sun, she looked at Connie and smiled to herself. *How kind of you to give me the whole morning off.* "She's a dental assistant." *Just get it over with.* "I met her when the company I worked for re-designed the office building where she worked. I spent a lot of time there, working on the design and ordering. We got to know each other a little, started eating lunch together a few times a week." She stopped, , and closed her eyes.

"How did she find out you were gay?"

You certainly can't let me stop now. "I told her. She

88

wanted me to go out with her to this hot spot for singles, so I told her."

"Was she shocked?"

"I think she was surprised, but she was also very curious." Kasey sat up and spread her fingers through her hair, which was drying now to lighter shades of gold. "She wanted to make a deal. I would go with her to this place she liked, and she in turn would go to a gay nightclub that I liked. I thought it was a pretty interesting idea, so I agreed."

Connie sat up next to her. "So what happened next?"

"We went to the singles bar. I was polite to the guys, but I turned down anyone who asked me to dance more than once. Cindy thought it was a cool idea, so she did too. It was an okay time. I realized I was definitely attracted to her. The next week we went to my club. We did the same thing there, only dancing with each woman once. Then I asked her to dance with me."

"And she did."

"Uh-huh, for the rest of the night. We'd both had a few drinks, and I kissed her for the first time while we were dancing."

"What'd she do?"

"Kissed me back. *I* was shocked. But I recovered quickly enough. It happened a number of times before we finally left and ended up at my place. She didn't leave until Monday morning. We were together for three years before the pressures became too much for her to handle. That was a little over two years ago."

"Anyone serious since then?" Connie realized she was beginning to sound like a talk show host, but she couldn't stop herself.

"Not really. Sharon's always trying to set me up, but I've never been interested in any of them."

"What kind of women are you attracted to?"

"That sounds like a *Dating Game* question."

There it was, the question over the limit. Connie was about to chastise herself when Kasey laughed.

"That would make an interesting show, wouldn't it? I'd have to choose between three beautiful women. Let's see. Number one has a great sense of humor, and number three loves to dance. But I like number two's self-confidence, wit, and sincerity. I'll take number two." She laughed more comfortably now. The ever-present tension she felt whenever she spoke of Cindy was gone. The inevitable, as Connie would call it, was over, and she was relieved. It was time to truly relax and to enjoy the heat of the sun, the hint of pine on the warm southern breeze, and her friend.

The flames of the fire cast their yellow glow in soft flickers around the little room. Basking in its warmth, Connie hummed softly with the strings of her guitar.

"How's your mom?" Kasey asked, joining her on the edge of the sofa.

"Dad said her signs are almost normal. They think it was some kind of stroke." Connie looked into Kasey's eyes. "I'll never be able to adequately thank you for all you've done. I think of you singing to Mom every morning. It means even more, now that I know about your own mother."

"To be honest with you, I think it was as much for me as it was for her. I couldn't sing to my own mom. I always cried. It felt good to be able to do that for yours. And then to know that she heard me..."

"How did your mom die?"

"Leukemia." Kasey dropped her eyes for a moment. "She was in so much pain for eight long weeks. Her skin hurt just to touch it. But she refused the morphine. She hated what it did to her mind." Tears began to fill Kasey's eyes as she spoke. "She said she could stand the pain. She didn't want to miss a minute of what was left."

Connie took her hand and held it tenderly. "You don't have to say any more, Kasey. I know it's painful."

"The memory's very painful, but I don't want to lose it either. I've never been able to tell anyone about it, especially her last words and the look on her face. I don't ever want to lose that." She blotted her eyes with the sleeve of her T-shirt but didn't stop talking. "She held her arms up to me, her hands shaking so, to try to touch my face. She wasn't strong enough, so I held her hands. She looked at me with such sweetness and said softly, 'You're so precious.'" Kasey's voice was quivering now. "I told her, *she* was precious to me, and she closed her eyes with a little smile. I never saw her eyes again. She lapsed into a coma about an hour later." Barely able to finish, Kasey whispered, "She died in my arms that night." The tears that filled her beautiful blue eyes were now spilling uncontrollably down her cheeks.

Connie pulled her close and embraced her, holding Kasey's head against her shoulder. She rocked her gently as she cried. "She must have loved you very much," Connie whispered. "Yes, she must have loved you very, very much."

FIFTEEN

"Isn't Friday your birthday?" Kasey asked, exiting the highway.

"If I count it."

"If you count it?"

"The big three-oh. I think it's time to call them something else."

Kasey smiled. It hadn't really occurred to her. Maybe at forty. "Got something special planned?"

"I told Mom we would celebrate my birthday and her

coming home at the same time. Dad thinks it could be another couple of weeks."

"You should still do something special on Friday, though. Would you like to go to dinner or a movie?"

"You really want to do something special for me on my birthday?"

"Of course. I wouldn't have asked if I didn't."

"Okay, take me to the nightclub."

Kasey tried masking her sudden annoyance the best she could. "What nightclub?"

She persisted. "The one you go to."

"No way, Connie. It's been a long time since I've even been there myself. Besides, why do you want to go there?" She stopped the car in Connie's drive.

"I just do. What's wrong with that?"

"I don't think it's a good idea. All you'd see would be a lot of women drinking and dancing together." Kasey was sorry now she had told her so much about Cindy. The whole idea smacked of dangerous curiosity.

"I want to know more about what it's like to be gay."

Exactly. Exactly why we aren't going. She needed her best diplomatic dissuasion here. "Connie, a night at the bar is not a true representation of gay life. You'll see them being themselves, able to hug and kiss, to dance with each other, and to talk openly. What's so deceiving is that most of them return to a double life the next day. Most of them can't be themselves at work, around family, or in public. It's totally misleading."

"Maybe it's important that I see both. I'm aware of how you present yourself in public and in business, and I've met Sharon. But I don't know many gay people." *It is a reasonable request. What is the big deal?*

Up until now, that forthright Connie Bradford approach to life had been quite enjoyable, but at the moment, it was irritating the hell out of Kasey. "You know Tom. He's a good example of how you can be associating with gay people every day and not realize it. We're just people, with hopes and dreams and fears like everyone else; except, we have to hide a very big part of who we are."

"What's the real reason you don't want to take me?"

Kasey stared at her for a few seconds. *Can I tell her how nervous that curiosity is making me? How frightening the similarity is? Or how sure I am about straight women not understanding society's pressures on gays until they live it themselves? No. Not right now. Not yet.*

Connie stared back for the next few seconds. "It could be a lot of fun, you know."

"Why am I always letting you talk me into things?"

"Because you like me?" Connie grinned.

"That must be it."

"What should I wear?"

"Whatever you'd wear out to a singles club. Are you ready to start running again tomorrow?"

"Yes." She was thrilled that Kasey had been the one to suggest it. "I've missed torturing you."

SIXTEEN

All week Connie felt as if she was operating in over-drive. Her mother continued to improve, gaining strength every day. With that relief, and her renewed energy from the weekend, she handled a full schedule and slept well every night. They found time to run three times, and she even had the patience to deal with Sharon's sarcasm. Kasey had been right. The weekend away had worked miracles.

Although she had been looking forward to tonight all week, Connie kept her excitement to herself. Twice she sensed Kasey wanted to back out of it. But she hadn't. And

Connie, insisting upon driving, picked her up without an argument.

They pulled into the club parking lot. "Nervous?" Kasey asked.

"A little. I just want to fit in and not look obvious. Are you sure I look okay?"

Kasey's eyes swept down the silk blouse and pants, all the way to the matching pumps. "You look great. Remember, if you don't want to dance with someone, all you have to do is say no. And I won't leave you sitting alone, okay?"

"Don't worry about me. Just enjoy yourself."

Connie scanned the sprawling room from their little table by the wall, while Kasey got their drinks. Lesbianism in truth, she decided, transcended race, religion, and class. It was no myth — a well-kept secret maybe, but no myth. She relaxed against the back of her chair. Kasey was absolutely right. Blending in really wasn't a concern. She made another pass over the crowd of women, stopping here and there on an interesting face, an intriguing combination. It was rare for her to be in the company of only women, and never in the sole company of so many. All of woman-kind seemed represented here, and it felt good to be among them.

She caught sight of Kasey emerging from the crowd near the bar and watched her squeeze through the crowd and maneuver gracefully between the tables. Her slender figure in tight black pants and short-waisted purple and black jacket turned heads as she passed. Connie was trying to decide whether she was sexier tonight than she was at the open house when Kasey's smile met her gaze. Never in her life had anyone intrigued her like this woman.

"You're turning heads."

"Then the trip was worth it." She smiled, placing their drinks on the table. "The dancers are here tonight."

Connie looked toward the dance floor. "Dancers?"

"A dance company that performs at different clubs. Something like the Chippendales, only they don't strip, and they dance for women. I think you'll like it. But be prepared, parts of it might get a little provocative."

"I liked Madonna's video."

Kasey grinned. "Ah, then I needn't worry."

Bright spots of purple and red suddenly illuminated the dance floor. Dancers, fit and lean in halter tops and shorts, began moving with the music. With choreographed precision, their bodies gave form and tactile sensuality to the music and interpreted it with an unusual emotional quality, a quality noticeably missing in the dancers Connie had seen performing for men. There were indeed parts that proved sensuous; the women touched each other and moved together in ways that simulated intimacy. They displayed an eroticism that merely alluded to sex, but stopped short of defining it. It wasn't at all what Connie had expected. She found herself not only appreciating the art of it, but enjoying it.

She glanced at Kasey. "Which one do you think is the sexiest?"

"Are you just trying to be one of the girls here?"

"No. I want to know what you think is sexy."

"You mean like dating material?"

"Sure. Would it be someone like one of the dancers?"

Kasey sighed and leaned back in her chair. "I guess the one in the black top wouldn't have to ask twice."

For the next few minutes Connie watched the woman that Kasey had indicated, noticing how physically feminine she was and how strong and confident her movements were. She was very attractive. Noticeable, too, was the eye contact she made with Kasey. The attraction was evidently mutual.

The performance ended with curves of women's bodies

intersecting and enveloping one another, while Kasey explained, "Between numbers the dancers mingle and dance with people. So if one approaches you and you don't want to dance, just shake your head no and she'll ask someone else."

"They actually mingle?" She watched Kasey nod. "When I went to a straight club that had dancers, the bouncers had to protect them and keep them separated from the men."

"No, this is much different. Women are much different." She had no sooner got the words out of her mouth, when the dancer in the black top approached their table.

"Good evening, ladies. I hope you're enjoying the show," she said before turning her attention to Kasey. She held out her hand, inviting her to dance.

Kasey hesitated. "Go ahead," encouraged Connie. "I've never seen you dance fast."

Kasey took her hand and stood. "Why don't you take off your jacket," the woman said. "I think you're going to get very warm."

She glanced quickly at Connie and back to the dancer. "Maybe so," she said as she removed her jacket. Underneath she wore a vestlike top that showed off her arms and shoulders and most of her back.

The woman boldly ran her hands across Kasey's broad shoulders and down her arms to her hands. "Are you single?" she asked.

"Yes. Are you?" asked Kasey, purposely turning the tables.

"I am now."

Barely a second passed, no time for a reaction, when a hand was extended in Connie's direction. She turned to see a dancer in white shorts and top smiling politely at her. Connie took the dancer's hand and followed her to the dance floor. It had been some time since she'd enjoyed dancing. Greg hated it. And she hadn't danced with a girl since junior high school. Now here she was in the middle of a gay bar doing both. She looked around for Kasey, wondering if she had seen her get up. She found her and her partner on the other side of the floor; the dancer was moving seductively, only inches separating them, looking directly into Kasey's eyes. The scene had an eroticism stronger than the performance. A flush swept swiftly over Connie's body. She watched them as discreetly as she could throughout the rest of the dance.

At the song's end, Connie thanked the dancer and anxiously made her way to the edge of the dance floor. All the while she kept Kasey in her sight and caught up with her as they neared the table.

"I'm glad you were comfortable enough to dance," Kasey smiled. "I didn't want to leave you sitting alone."

"I was surprised when she asked me."

"Why would you be surprised? You're a beautiful woman, Connie. I hope you realize there are going to be more invitations tonight. I hope it won't bother you."

"I don't think it will."

During the next performance Kasey was acutely aware that Connie's eyes were fixed on her, studying her, practically ignoring the dancers. *If she is trying to be discreet, she certainly isn't very good at it. If she isn't trying* . . . Kasey slyly turned to look at her. "What do you think of the dancers?"

"They're very good. Are they all gay?"

"I think most of them are. I'm glad they don't offend you."

"Why would they?"

"I don't know. I guess I assume straight people have a hard time, at least at first, seeing gay people touching each other."

Before the conversation could go any further and before the dancers could even clear the floor, two women approached their table. From the way they moved and the way they were dressed, Kasey knew exactly what was about to happen. One of them asked, "Would you ladies like to dance?"

Kasey waited, looking at Connie for her response. When she stood, Kasey followed suit. They danced to a number of fast songs, all with different women, before finally retreating to the table for a break. But Connie had barely caught her breath when a woman dressed casually in jeans and leather vest asked her to dance. She'd danced a fast one with her earlier, but this time it was a slow song. She looked quickly over at Kasey before accepting. A smile eased across Kasey's face as Connie stood.

It was the first time she had ever danced slow with a woman, and she knew exactly why she had accepted. Somehow, she was sure it would prove to Kasey that she was indeed accepting of her lifestyle. Besides, she really was enjoying herself. It was refreshingly different. Absent were the constant sexual innuendoes, the unwelcome pursuit. Absent too, was the discomfort of unending decisions of which comments to challenge and which ones to grit your teeth and bear. No wonder women loved women.

The woman was holding Connie close, but not uncomfortably so; their bodies barely touched. They were talking about it being Connie's first time at the club and how much they liked the performances. Then something caught Connie's eye. The dancer in black and Kasey were dancing not far from them. They were hardly moving. The dancer stared deeply into Kasey's eyes. She was following the slow, graceful movements with her arms around Kasey's neck. The vision was undeniably sexy the way their bodies came together, the way their eyes made contact. Connie found herself staring and forced herself to look elsewhere. As she glanced around the floor, watching other couples as they danced, she began to get a better idea of what lesbian couples looked like. Her preconceived idea of the masculine-feminine combination wasn't entirely accurate. Some couples were both quite masculine, some were somewhere in between. But it became apparent too that a couple as feminine as Kasey and the dancer were a definite minority. Her attention was drawn to them once again. This time she allowed herself to watch to the end of the song. She liked the feeling it gave her.

Her obsession with Kasey had caused her to practically ignore her dance partner. "I'm sorry I haven't been very good company. I've got a lot on my mind right now."

"That's okay," the woman replied as they parted. "Maybe we can dance again."

Back at the table alone, Connie had a minute to think. She hadn't meant to be rude or inattentive. But this obsession was unrelenting. It made her very warm. It filled her with anxiety. At times she was even uncomfortable. Yet she didn't want to be anywhere else or with anyone else. All she wanted, she realized, was to be the one in Kasey's arms.

Kasey's voice startled her from her thoughts. "I see you survived your first slow dance."

"Did you doubt I would?"

"Not that you would survive it, maybe that you would enjoy it."

"She wouldn't have been my first choice, but it was enjoyable enough." She waited for a reply that never came, while Kasey sipped her drink and surveyed the crowd in silence. *Was she looking for the dancer in black? Thinking about her?* Patience, even with Kasey, waned. "Tell me something," Connie said. "Assuming everyone in here is gay and single" — her eyes held Kasey's —"which one would you most want to dance with?"

Kasey looked down at her glass, swirling the ice cubes around for what seemed like a long time. Connie watched her. Kasey was pensive, serious. Then she looked up at

Connie again. Connie had not seen that expression before. It made her heart jump. Without a word, Kasey stood and held out her hand.

Connie's heart leaped as she looked into her eyes. "I thought you'd never ask."

Taking her hand, Connie let Kasey lead her to the dance floor and take her in her arms. The sense of intimacy as her breasts pressed between Kasey's and her forehead touched the side of her face surpassed any she had ever felt. Beyond the hugs of a friend, as tight as they could be, and deeper than the sincerest tears, their embrace said something that had never been said. And suddenly everything was very clear. Connie was in love with Kasey Hollander. The signs had been there for a long time: uncomfortable anxiety whenever they were apart for more than a day, her heart pounding the beat of a school-girl crush, and the incredible shocks of electricity shooting magically from the blue eyes to the center of her. Everything she should have felt for a man and never did. She felt that, and more, for this woman with emotions so like her own. *She* was the reason for the fullness in her heart, and why there was no emptiness. Yes, Kasey had touched her heart. Connie found herself playing back the words to the song Kasey had sung with Tom. No, no one had ever touched her heart like this before.

A lesbian is a woman who falls in love with another woman. Kasey's own prophetic words. It didn't matter what anyone called her love for Kasey. It was there and she would not deny it.

She had not given a lot of conscious effort to understanding love in the past. She assumed such things took care of themselves; love would happen when it happened, and you would know it when it was there. Statistics, tax bases, percentiles — those were the things that took analytical thought and that she was quite good at. Applying the same process to matters of the heart, however, proved to be a slow, ineffective approach. No wonder it took so long to figure out what her heart was saying. All along, the empty places she had ignored for so long were being filled naturally as she fell in love. What she had to do now was figure out how she was going to tell Kasey.

Shyness not being one of her own shortcomings, she pulled Kasey's hand around to the small of her back and placed her own hand on the back of Kasey's neck. As she leaned the full length of her body against her, Kasey's arms tightened around her and she felt a warm surge of electricity. Kasey's heart pounding hard against her chest and her face gently nuzzling against Connie's made one thing obvious — the physical attraction was mutual. The feel of Kasey's body moving against her own began to make her warm. The temptation was to tell her now, but she didn't want anything to change this moment. She wanted to enjoy this feeling as long as possible. Closing her eyes, she pressed her lips against Kasey's neck.

As the music tapered off, she whispered, "There's something I have to tell you." Kasey released her embrace and looked directly into Connie's eyes. Connie hesitated, fixed on the blueness. Something kept the words from coming out. Maybe fear, maybe being in the middle of the dance floor. Nevertheless, before the words could be said, someone interrupted her chance. A hand on her arm brought her attention to one of the women who had asked her to dance. "Hey, why didn't you just say you two were together? It's cool," she said with a big smile.

There was silence until they reached the table. "The smoke's starting to get to me. Would you mind if we start for home?" Kasey asked.

"No, that's fine. It is awfully thick."

They picked up their things. Kasey once again covered her wonderful body with her jacket, and they started for the exit.

They were stopped before reaching the door by the

woman in jeans that Connie had danced the slow dance with. With her arm around Connie's waist, she slipped a piece of paper into her hand and whispered something in her ear. Kasey, already halfway out the door, looked back just as the woman kissed Connie on the cheek. Kasey hesitated, but when Connie smiled and said something in return, Kasey decided it was nothing to worry about. Seconds later, Connie was out the door right behind her.

"Hey, hot stuff," Kasey smiled. "I thought I was going to have to come and get you."

"I never expected some woman's phone number tonight," she said, handing the paper to Kasey.

"Don't give it to me; she's not my type."

"Well, I told her I've got a girlfriend."

"What? You heartbreaker."

"Better now than later, I always say."

Kasey laughed and shook her head. "And I was worried about you? Silly me."

"Listen, you weren't Miss Innocence all night, so don't even pretend. You know how those women were looking at you. They were probably just too intimidated to offer their phone numbers."

"No, they did."

"Really? So what did you tell them?"

"That I was entering a convent next week."

Connie burst out laughing at the thought, and Kasey joined her. "So what'd they say?"

"They wanted to know which one."

Their laughter was good, a release of tension and a gentle erasure of worry. It filled a healthy portion of their time together, along with everything else they shared. Their relationship had all the right ingredients, and they both recognized it. And now for Connie, the revelation of love had made it perfect. But she was as nervous as she was excited.

"I haven't even wished you a happy birthday yet,"

exclaimed Kasey, as they stopped in her drive. She reached into a bag on the floor and handed Connie a small narrow box. "Happy birthday."

"Kasey, taking me to the club was enough. You shouldn't have got me anything."

"I love to give presents. So humor me."

When Connie saw the gold bracelet, she replied quietly, "Kasey, it's beautiful."

"Here, put it on." Kasey fastened the clasp, locking the bracelet around Connie's wrist.

"I know you spent too much, but I love it."

Kasey looked up just as Connie leaned forward. Without warning Connie kissed her tenderly on the lips. Despite her heart trying to jump from her chest, she gave Kasey no time to react. She grasped the back of her neck and carefully pulled their lips together again. There was no resistance. Kasey's mouth was warm and smelled of alcohol and spearmint. Her lips were sensuous and soft, yielding to the gentle pressure of Connie's mouth. She was kissing her, as Kasey said, the way she had always wanted to be kissed. And as she did so Kasey parted her lips, yielding completely. She had never felt anything as sexual, had never been so aroused. She entered, tasted the warm wetness with her tongue, and explored her gently. Then pressing her open mouth against Kasey's, she invited her in, along with the ache that had begun deep in her abdomen. Connie felt the velvety touch of Kasey's tongue, felt her move into her, felt the touch of her hand on her thigh. Excitement was overtaking her, awakening her senses to a brilliance she'd never known. For the first time in her life she wanted sex, and she wanted it with Kasey. The kiss began to take on a life of its own, her senses gaining the edge of control. And that was okay. She had never felt this good. Then, in a transition, when their lips were barely touching, Connie whispered, "I'm in love with you."

Abruptly, as if slapped into reality, Kasey pulled back.

Her eyes darkened with fear. "No, Connie, no," she whispered. "You can't — *I* can't."

Before there was time to respond, Kasey bolted from the car like a frightened deer, leaving Connie shocked and confused. Connie leaned her head back against the seat and tried to clear her mind. Her body, warm and wet, still felt the effects of their kisses. "What? What?" she asked aloud.

Minutes went by, she didn't know how many, before she finally drove home. If her interpretation was correct, she'd just been rejected, and it felt terrible. No wonder men hated it. It made her remember the dream she used to have as a young girl. In the dream, she was always somewhere public when suddenly she would realize that she was naked from the waist up. Desperately she would try to cover herself with her arms, and escape the laughing faces. It left her feeling embarrassed and stupid for being in that position. Just like now. Yet despite her embarrassment, the one person she found herself needing to talk to about it was Kasey. She was, in fact, her best friend. And nothing was going to change that.

SEVENTEEN

Spending most of Saturday and Sunday with her family at the hospital helped pass the time. Connie tried calling Kasey late into the night, both nights, with no luck. Time wasn't making it any easier. Even the strings of her guitar held no solace. Her fingers missed their mark, lost their place. She tried to think, but thinking only brought tears. Work today had been difficult at best.

She dialed Kasey's number again. To her surprise, Kasey answered on the second ring. "Hi," Connie greeted, trying to sound casual. "I tried to call all weekend."

"I was at the cabin. I needed some time alone. How's your mom?"

"She's doing pretty good. Her voice is getting a little stronger. We all spent the weekend with her."

"I'm sorry I didn't get up to see her today."

"She asked where her angel was."

"I missed seeing her, too. I'll go up tomorrow."

An uncomfortable silence followed. Connie waited. She wanted Kasey to be the first to bring it up, but the silence continued. Finally Connie said, "Can we get together and talk?"

"I think we should give it a little more time. I'll give you a call later in the week. Okay?"

"If that's what you want." She hesitated. "I'll miss you. Have a good week."

"You too."

Connie lay back on the bed and stared at the ceiling. She was sure it was wiser not to let Kasey know how upset she was, not to chance an even worse reaction. But nothing so far in her life had prepared her for the situation she found herself in now. Falling in love with a woman certainly had not been in her future plans, and it seemed dealing with that should be enough. Her coping skills did not include dealing with Kasey's reaction. The possibility that Kasey was not in love with her was real and almost unbearable. But if that was the case, she would have to find a way to keep her best friend and make her heart behave. Whatever it took.

EIGHTEEN

Troy stopped in the hallway of the new job site, a column of light fixture boxes balanced in his arms. "Sharon, where does Kasey want these?"

"I don't know, Troy. You'd better ask her. You don't want to put them in the wrong room today."

"Where is she?"

Before Sharon could answer, Kasey's voice resonated from the kitchen, "Dammit!" Sharon raised her eyebrows and pointed.

"Gotcha," he grinned.

"Kase, where do you want these fixtures?"

"I don't really care, Troy. On the roof if you like," she replied from under the sink. "This whole damn thing has to be ripped out."

"Something I can do to help?"

"Yeah, light a match to this place."

"Hey, maybe it's time for a break," he suggested, setting the boxes down.

"Sorry," she grumbled, crawling out from under the sink. "I haven't had any patience all week."

Hesitantly he asked, "Is this *that* week of the month?"

"No. Bet you can't wait 'til that week."

"Listen, Kase, maybe it's none of my business, but it's been obvious all week that something's wrong. You may think you keep your feelings to yourself, but you don't. We can tell by your moods and by the way you work around here if you're happy or sad ... or mad. The only thing you keep to yourself is why. Maybe it would help if you just told somebody."

Without looking at him she tossed the wrench under the sink. "You're right," she said, leaving the room. "It's none of your business."

Sharon looked out the side door on her way to the kitchen and stopped when she saw Kasey at the tailgate of the truck. She headed for the driveway to help, but as she came around the front of the truck, she could see that Kasey was resting her head on folded arms on the top of the tailgate. "Kase," Sharon said, reaching out to gently massage the back of Kasey's neck. "You okay?"

Kasey spoke into the space between her chest and the tailgate. "I just snapped at Troy for no reason." After a pause, she lifted her head. "I know I've been rough to work with all week. I'm sorry."

"Anything I can do to help?"

"No, I'll just have to work things out myself. I don't mean to take things out on you two. It's just been a helluva week."

"I know you don't want to hear it again, but I think it would do you a world of good to come to the party tomorrow night. You don't socialize enough. You need to get outside yourself a little bit and have fun."

"I know, I know. I'll think about it. Thanks for understanding." She straightened her posture and opened the tailgate. "Guess we'd better get back to work."

NINETEEN

Connie crammed as much into three days and three nights as was humanly possible. She wanted no empty time, no spaces for thought. Keeping busy until she was totally exhausted was the only way she could sleep. A calm and logical mind failed when thoughts of Kasey were triggered. The combination of stresses and lack of sleep taxed her stamina and emotional strength, and once again she found herself completely drained. Her patience was thin, her tolerance low.

How long she could maintain patience with Kasey she

didn't know. Her anxiety was at an all-time high. She fought being angry with her. She needed desperately to talk to her.

The loud ringing of the telephone next to her head startled her. The sound of Kasey's voice increased her heartbeat even more.

Kasey's voice was soft and clear. "How are you?"

"Not good. How about you?"

"Not much better."

"Tell me what you've been thinking." There was a pause. "Kasey, I can't take not talking to you."

Finally, "We crossed the line, Connie. There's no changing it or pretending it didn't happen."

"I don't want to pretend it didn't happen. I know how I feel, Kasey."

Kasey's voice rose a level, gained firmness. "You have no idea what being a lesbian is all about, Connie. What you saw at the club is not the true picture. I tried to tell you that. It's not that easy."

"It doesn't matter what it entails. The truth is, I cannot deny how I feel. That's impossible for me. I will just learn to live as a lesbian."

"You're so damn naive! Think about what could happen if your family found out, or your boss. Look what happened when Greg only suspected. Do you want to deal with reactions like that for the rest of your life?"

"No, I don't want to. But it isn't really a choice. Is it?" There was only silence from Kasey's end. When she couldn't stand it any longer, Connie asked, "Are you going to honestly tell me how you feel about me?"

Continued silence. Connie resisted saying anything more. After a few more uncomfortable seconds, Kasey cleared her throat. *Has she been crying?* "Kasey, I've got to see you."

Kasey's voice was soft once again. "No, not for a while. We both need some time."

Tears were now running down Connie's face. "Please, Kasey. I'll do anything you want. We'll just be friends again. Please, promise me you won't give up on our friendship."

The voice on the other end wavered noticeably. "It could never be the same."

Connie struggled through her tears. "Do you love me?"

"Don't . . ."

"I'll wait" — her voice barely escaped now through a quickly tightening throat — "for you to call." Connie heard the click at the other end and hung up. "I love you," she whispered, then buried her face in the pillow and cried.

TWENTY

Through the charcoal grayness of nightfall, Kasey watched the figures of the women as they made their way around the cars in front of Sharon's house. She didn't know how many women had passed since she had arrived. And she wasn't sure why it was so difficult for her to get out of the car. They weren't strangers. Most of these women she knew, except for Sharon's friends from New York. But it had been a long time since she'd been to a party. Maybe enough time had gone by for everyone to forget about the state of her love life. She hoped so. She didn't want it to be an issue tonight.

She sat there. Unable to move. Unable to stop the thought of showing up tonight hand in hand with Connie Bradford. Unable to keep from wondering. The reaction would not be the one they had received at the club, that they were single and available. *These* women knew her. They would know, once again, she had fallen for a straight woman. And reactions on the whole would not be good. There were very few who understood Kasey Hollander. Even fewer understood what attracted her — those self-assured qualities wrapped in such a neat, feminine package. Most believed as Sharon, that feminine-looking lesbians are copping out and only playing the "hetero game." And Kasey knew she was included in that category, blending into society as easily as she did. After all these years, Sharon's major source of contention was still Kasey's unwillingness to come out. They would never even have become friends had Sharon not fallen in love with her.

Making matters even worse was her friends' view of heterosexual women: selfish, dependent, shallow excuses of women, promising only frustration and emotional pain of the worst kind. Reasons much too often valid. Tonight though, she didn't need to hear them.

Actually, Kasey was the exception to many of Sharon's rules, as was noted by many of their friends. Sharon merely told them, "Showing the world you can build a house with the very same hands you apply your lipstick with is as powerful as telling them who shares your bed." Privately though, the pressure was always there to come out.

Unwilling yet to leave the anonymity of her sanctuary, Kasey flipped down the visor mirror and whisked her fingers swiftly through the wisps of hair framing her face until she was satisfied with their placement. *So what's so wrong with a little makeup and a flattering hairstyle? And*

116

what's the crime in dressing up traditional male qualities in a congenial personality and fashionable clothes? The results are all that count, right? All in all, she was pretty comfortable with herself. She liked the fact that people usually accepted her at face value, without undue scrutiny. She was good at comfortable conversations with almost anyone, and as it should be, her sexuality was rarely an issue. Admittedly, wearing her mother's diamond on her engagement finger was a cop-out. But what it did to discourage unwanted advances was worth it, she rationalized. Kasey the woman had come a long way from the withdrawn little tomboy who had struggled only for permission to develop her whole self, who had floated in oblivion between a part of society that rejected her strengths and desires and another that questioned her needs and tastes. And all the while she needed acceptance from both. Yet it had been an empowering journey. And somewhere along the way she had come to believe that the world must not be allowed to relate to a woman by who shares her bed — male *or* female.

Objective? Maybe not. But then, neither was Sharon. Sharon did, however, know how to throw one hell of a party. And she might be right about its therapeutic value. If nothing else, it would get Connie off her mind for at least tonight. She might even meet someone else. *What the hell.* She finally emerged from her metal refuge. *Just do it.*

Sharon's ex answered the door. Not a surprise. Sharon and Sue had remained good friends. "Well, look who's here," she exclaimed, giving Kasey a breath-excising hug. "Sharon said you might show up tonight."

"I guess it's about time, eh?"

"I'll say. Everyone's downstairs. I'll be down shortly. Get something to drink and *mingle.*"

* * * * *

117

Dressed in black spandex pants, a silk tank top, and black jacket, Kasey worked her way through the crowd of familiar and unfamiliar faces. Amid whispers and surprised greetings, she smiled and talked her way across the huge basement toward Sharon. She was only a couple of people away when one of the women talking with Sharon noticed her.

As deep brown eyes concentrated on her own, she overheard her say, "Be still my heart, *who* is *this*?"

Sharon turned, a proud smile spreading across her face. "Mmm, baby, you look delicious," she said, grabbing Kasey in a bear hug.

"Behave yourself," Kasey laughed.

"Only when I have to."

"Well, you have to. Are you going to introduce me?"

"Of course. This is Kelly, and Pat. They're visiting this week from New York. And this is Sage. She's leaving the Big Apple and moving here. I invited her to stay with me until she gets settled. Everyone, this is Kasey, my best friend and business associate."

For the next half hour Kasey listened to college reminiscences and tales of New York, while the woman with the intriguing eyes and unusual name made her interest known. With mannered ease, Sage Bristo offered at-your-elbow attention, servicing Kasey with a drink, something to eat, and an intent ear. No one had to tell Kasey that Sage couldn't take her eyes off her. She could feel her eyes registering every detail, even when someone else was speaking. The attention was flattering, and despite the fact that Sage was more masculine than she liked, she had to admit the woman oozed with sensuality. She was tall and meticulously groomed, with the confidence of an aristocrat, and her appeal was undeniable. The interest Kasey felt was unintentional. Her own evaluation was discreetly sweeping over the short brown waves when an arm slid neatly around her waist. A turn of her head put her cheek to cheek with Sharon's ex.

"When was the last time you danced with a handsome dyke?" Sue asked.

With a laugh she answered, "It's been a while."

"Come on then, dance with me," she said, taking her hand.

Through two songs they danced and talked, and the whole while Sage Bristo watched. When Sage met Kasey with another drink at the end of the dance, Kasey kept them moving, introducing Sage to others, enjoying the attention. She was aware of thinking about Connie maybe only a half dozen times, which was definitely an improvement. Connie Bradford had dominated too much of her time, she decided. All day as she worked, all night as she lay awake, revisiting the sight of her, hearing her voice, tasting her lips. She shook the thoughts from her mind immediately, sharply turning her head in an abrupt decisiveness. There would be no time for that tonight, and that was fine.

"How about a dance with another handsome dyke?" Sage asked.

Quietly she answered, "I normally lead, but . . . sure."

"I haven't met a woman yet who couldn't follow me," she said, taking Kasey in her arms. Her form was classically correct and her words true to their promise.

"You're not dating Sharon, are you?" she asked.

"No. We've been close friends for a long time."

"Are you dating anyone else?"

She knew before the question where this was going. "No again."

"I'm very attracted to you." There was a slight hesitation as Sage tried to make eye contact. "I'd like to date you."

Kasey finally complied, only briefly, then looked away. "I'm usually not attracted to —"

"A handsome dyke with a great personality, her own business, and a fondness for dancing?" She flashed a big smile and gently squeezed Kasey's waist. Sage had sensed Kasey's discomfort and was easing gracefully out of it.

"Maybe we should get to know each other a little better."

"Not a problem. I just want you to know how I feel."

Sharon found them at the end of their dance. "Hey, Kase, Jan brought her keyboard. Will you sing?"

"I don't know, Sharon. You know what happened last time," Kasey reminded her. The memory of breaking down in the middle of "I Will Always Love You" was all too vivid.

"Don't sing that one. Besides it's been long enough that you'll be all right. Come on, please?"

"I'll lead, if everyone sings, okay?"

"Okay, come on. Jan's getting set up." Sharon took her hand. They made their way to the end of the room where the removal of a partition had left a platform perfect for entertainment.

Warm-up chords drifted into "Pretty Woman" over the open microphone, and everyone's attention was on the three women at the end of the room. "Here we go," announced Sharon.

With Kasey's strong, clear voice leading, the crowd of women was soon enjoying song after song. Sometime after the first song, but well before the fourth, the old familiar comfort returned. Kasey began to enjoy herself. And it didn't go unnoticed. "We want Kasey to sing," shouted someone in the back. Others joined the effort, calling her name and yelling out requests.

Sharon hovered over Jan and whispered something in her ear, then looked at Kasey. "C'mon, Kase," she said, as Jan began "No One Else on Earth," Sharon's favorite song.

Kasey stepped back to the microphone and relented. "Okay, okay." The beat quickly found its attitude in the way it drifted and pulsed from one part of her body to the next.

Then she jumped in full voice, right on cue and let 'em have it.

Between verses she strutted from Jan to the microphone and back, the sweat running down the sides of her face. Before returning to the microphone for the second verse, she removed her jacket to expose arms and shoulders reserved for these women's eyes. And they loved it. Whistles pierced the air. They shouted and cheered and made the most of their chance to openly let this woman know how appealing she was to them. And Kasey, the entertainer, was unmerciful. She strutted back to the keyboard, draped her jacket around Jan's shoulders, and seductively kissed her neck. Head tilted back in submission, Jan closed her eyes, and the women lost all reasonable control.

"Goddamn, she's hot," Sage exclaimed to the women around her.

"Yeah. It's too bad she likes straight women," replied one. "There's more than a couple of broken-hearted dykes out here."

"A lipstick lesbian with het cravings," added another.

"You don't like her," Sage assumed, not taking her eyes from the intriguing Kasey.

"We love her. We just wish she'd come to her senses. She went into hiding after her last lover left her for a man."

Before the applause died, Jan was already into another intro, giving Kasey little choice but to step to the microphone once again, this time to offer her own rendition of Lorrie Morgan's "Watch Me."

Toward the end of the song, Sharon appeared beside the platform with a towel. "For Kasey," she explained to Sage.

"Why don't you let me give it to her?"

"Go for it. But, I have to warn you —"

"I've already been warned."

Kasey replaced the microphone on its stand despite pleas from the women for another song. "My throat is dry," she explained, prompting an immediate offer of a dozen drinks. "Let me take a break, and then I'll do one more."

Her top was soaked, and the hair against her face and neck was dark blond with perspiration. She was met with a towel, a fresh drink, and Sage. "Oh, *thank* you," she said, blotting her face with the towel.

"You can really sing. And you haven't made a career of it?" Sage asked, watching the towel sweep over Kasey's arms and chest.

"How many lesbians do you know who've made a career singing?"

"Uh, two?"

"I know of four. It's too hard a life, in or out of the closet."

"Not having to share you with the world has its appeal. But that kind of talent should never be hidden."

Kasey smiled. "I enjoy singing for friends." The drink went down a little too easily. She knew she should be drinking water. "Well, I promised one more. I'll be back shortly." Kasey handed Sage the towel and started for the platform. But Sage's eyes wouldn't release their gaze as she pressed the towel to her lips. Kasey smiled and shook her head.

Amid cheers and clapping, Kasey leaned over to Jan, then picked up the microphone once again. "This one's one of *my* favorites. Some people think it was written especially for me." A few soft laughs accompanied the beginning notes to Patsy Cline's famous "Crazy." Her hands gripped the microphone, her eyes closed softly, and her voice delivered itself from her soul. Grateful hearts took it in. Women embracing one another swayed with her emotion, sang softly with her, cared from a place deep inside themselves.

Tears welled in Sharon's eyes at the sight of the glistening trail on Kasey's cheeks. Her voice stayed strong though, and she finished the last stanza with no indication that there was a problem. The women clapped long and hard for Kasey and Jan as they made their way out into the party again. Sharon grasped her hand as she passed. Kasey squeezed it reassuringly. "I'm okay. I'll be back in a few."

Once outside she took in a long deep breath of air and closed her eyes. Before she could exhale she lost her balance and had to lean heavily on the railing to keep from falling. With both hands on the top rail, she kept her eyes open and tried again. *That's better.* Carefully she lowered herself to the steps where she could gather her bearings and do a little thinking. Neither was an easy task. *Isn't the whole purpose of tonight not to think?* She wiped the dampness from her cheeks. She didn't want to cry, and she didn't want to think. Thinking only confused matters lately, anyway. Make a mistake once, and it can be chalked up to ignorance; make the same one again, and it reeks of stupidity. Ergo, falling in love with Connie would be stupid, plain and simple. Head cradled uncomfortably between the hard cold spindles of the railing, Kasey once again closed her eyes. *You will not go through that again.* That reminder needed emphasis. *You will never . . . ever . . . go through that again.*

A few more minutes and a number of deep breaths later, she headed back to the party.

"There you are," Sage exclaimed. "I was hoping I could have another dance."

Kasey took her hand. "Sure."

She was grateful for a slow one. Her legs felt suddenly unsteady. Sage began holding her at the respectable distance of their first dance. But it didn't take Kasey long to realize just how unsteady she was. She put both arms around Sage's shoulders and pressed up against her. Sage responded by wrapping her arms around her waist and moving very slowly. Much easier, Kasey thought hazily. Leaning her head against Sage's, she hummed along with the music and allowed her mind to go blank. She didn't even know how long it had been before she became aware of Sage's hands caressing her back. Since there were no objections, she kissed the side of Kasey's face, then the sweet saltiness of her neck. Kasey's eyes remained closed while she stroked the back of Sage's head and neck and pressed warm lips into her neck. Kasey felt Sage's arms tighten around her and soft lips move from her earring to her earlobe.

"If you're trying to turn me on," Sage whispered, "you've succeeded."

Kasey lifted her head, her lips less than an inch from Sage's, and looked directly into her eyes. The invitation couldn't be ignored. Sage lowered her eyes and kissed her tenderly. Once. Twice. With lips soft and full. The kiss was returned with Kasey tightening her embrace around Sage's shoulders and parting her lips. Their warm and tender exploration quickly turned passionate. Sage continued to move with the music, gathering Kasey tighter to her.

The burning deep within surprised Kasey. "Mmm," she murmured, burying her face in Sage's neck and gently caressing the back of her head.

Confidently, Sage's hands moved over Kasey's hips and buttocks, encouraging their seductiveness. "You're incredible," she whispered, brushing her lips over Kasey's cheek before meeting her mouth passionately once again. They were kissing deeply when the song ended. Kasey's hand firmly held the back of her neck, indicating no desire to stop. Sage eased their passion into tender touches of their lips and whispered, "Come upstairs with me."

For a second or two, Kasey tried to raise adequate reason not to, but none came to mind. She took Sage's hand and followed her unsteadily up the stairs.

In a darkened hallway, in the arms of a seductive Sage Bristo, Kasey Hollander allowed a long-suppressed part of herself its freedom once again. She let hands, unafraid of their power, venture over her until her body radiated heat. She allowed accomplished lips to spark a desire that surged through her body, a desire that needed no confirmation of love, that demanded only continuation. Freely Kasey matched Sage kiss for kiss. Their hips, sliding neatly together, fanned the heat of an undeniable ache. Kasey slipped her hand beneath the open buttons at the top of Sage's shirt and realized how much she missed the feel of warm smooth skin. Thought would not be allowed to alter this course. Not tonight. Not as long as it was this easy, this uncomplicated.

"We need to go into my room," Sage whispered against her ear. "It's right behind me."

A given, really, at this point. Yet Kasey moved only to bring them together in still another deep kiss. Sage's hands unfastening her bra felt wonderful, moving warmly over her back, sliding boldly around to cover her breasts. Her leg was lifted up and around Sage's thigh while Sage's lips traveled the curve of her throat to the base of her neck. The low moan she heard was her own, flowing free as her head tilted backward in a dizzy heat. "Let me take you the rest of the way," Sage whispered hot against Kasey's chest. "Let me taste you."

Kasey's eyes flashed open with a start. She pressed Sage against the door in a firm embrace, resting her forehead against the flat plane of Sage's jaw. "I can't make love with you."

"What is it you think we've been doing?"

"I'm drunk, Sage," she said, focusing hazily into the brown eyes. "This isn't love."

"Does it matter, if it feels this good?"

"Yes," she said, pulling from Sage's arms.

Carefully Kasey made her way downstairs in search of her confidante. She found her headed toward the stairs.

"I was just coming to see if you were all right."

"Sharon . . . I . . . need to talk to you."

"You, my dear, are drunk. I've never seen you drink this much."

Kasey put her arms around her friend's neck and rested against her forehead. "I'm in love, Sharon."

"With me?" she smiled.

"I've always loved you."

"I know, I know, just not that way. Then I hope you mean Sage."

Kasey lifted her head. She focused slowly on her friend.

Sharon tilted her head. The look was concern, pure and sincere. "No, Kasey. Not again. What am I going to do with you?"

Kasey put her head down on Sharon's shoulder and let her hold her for a while. "You're staying here tonight," Sharon said firmly. "Come on, let's make it up these steps one more time."

TWENTY-ONE

Connie replaced the handset on the phone for the third time in the last five minutes. She hadn't completed Kasey's number once. With a deep breath she tilted her head back, placed her hands on her hips, and made her tenth or twelfth trip to the front window. The little calico from next door lifted her black Chaplin mustache and gave a loud greeting. It was way past time for her usual morning smelt treat. She stretched an orange-and-white paw up as far as she could reach and pressed it against the glass. Connie turned away from the window.

No diversion worked anymore. Thoughts of Kasey now

consumed Connie's every minute. Every anxious moment that she was away from her made more and more of Connie's life unimportant. The fear that she tried so hard not to give in to was looking more and more like reality. She may have lost Kasey.

She walked aimlessly from room to room searching for a way to cope. There had to be some positive move she could make, however small, something that would give back some semblance of control in her life. She needed to talk to someone, and there was only one choice.

She strode up the walk of the large Tudor-style home and was greeted by a nice-looking man dressed in summer slacks and shirt. "You must be Connie," he offered with a handshake. "I'm Michael. Just on my way out to run errands. Tom's expecting you," he smiled. "Go on in."

Tom appeared from a doorway, wiping his hands on a kitchen towel, as she stepped into the cool tiled entranceway. "Come on," he motioned. "I'll only bore you with the nickel tour. It doesn't include before and after slides or market analysis."

They wandered through the huge house while Tom pointed out where Kasey had done the remodeling, and Connie revisited the warmth of Kasey's embrace. There were furnishings of period pieces and antiques. Some had been inherited, some purchased, all with interesting stories attached. His knowledge was notable, and his enjoyment in having found certain pieces would have been contagious if her mind weren't so preoccupied. Despite the fact that her own taste leaned toward the contemporary, she appreciated the interest and effort that must have gone into such a project. Today, though, wasn't a good day to show her appreciation.

"Your home is a showpiece, Tom," she said as they settled on the couch. "It's really beautiful."

"I must admit that Michael and I enjoyed the fun and exciting part while Kasey did the hard work. But this isn't taking care of why you're here. I didn't mean to take up so much time with a tour."

"I did enjoy it, Tom. Ordinarily I'd be better company." Her eyes wandered out the window and then came back to his. "I have a confession to make. Even with the hours we spent practicing together, I didn't know much about you. And I was curious."

"I could tell from the questions you were asking at the open house," he said with a smile. "But that wasn't the only reason you were asking, was it?"

"No. But at the time, I didn't even understand why. It wasn't until last weekend that I finally put it all together." She hesitated, but didn't pull her eyes away. "I realized that I'm in love with her."

In the middle of a wide smile, Tom exclaimed, "I knew it!"

"God, I must be slow. Can I just tell you what has happened, without any of my thoughts on it, and you give me an objective view of the situation?"

"I'll try."

In the amount of time that it would take to wash and dry the dinner dishes, Connie outlined her entire relationship with Kasey Hollander. Amazing how something so easily encapsulated could have such an absolute effect over the whole of your life. Stripped of descriptive emotion, it appeared by most standards to be merely a grouping of ordinary encounters. A diminutive span, hardly capable of mending a life's worth of broken dreams or filling a lifetime of empty places. Yet it seemed it could do just that. And as hard as she tried against it, her factual account began to take on emotion, at first reflected in her face, as a flush accompanied her confession of love, and then shown in the unconstrained tears as she recounted their last conversation.

Tom reached over and took her hand. "Sweetie, you're in deep."

She looked at him, his handsome face blurred with her tears. Her voice was soft. "I know."

"And so is she," he added as he left the room. He returned with a box of Kleenex.

Her heart charged with possibility. "What do you mean?"

"She's in love with you. I've thought so since the open house. I even asked her about it, but of course she denied it."

"Were we that obvious?"

"To me, and I understand to your Neanderthal, too, if you don't mind my candor." He watched Connie smile and finish dabbing her eyes dry. "Neither one of you could take your eyes off the other. And the emotion when she sang . . ."

"It gave me goose bumps."

"It should have," he smiled. "It was for you."

"If she is in love with me, why is she denying it?"

"It's taken Kasey a long time to get healthy again, after Cindy. I'm sure the fact that you've lived straight all your life frightens her. We were close friends during the years she and Cindy were together. In fact, they wouldn't be seen together in public unless Michael and I were with them. I saw what it did to her, Connie." He leaned toward her, rested his forearms on his knees. "Trying to please Cindy only made her nervous and paranoid. She gave her heart and soul to that woman, and she left her devastated."

"She must have lost her mother around the same time."

"Within months, the two most important people in her

life were gone." With words as direct as his eye contact, he asked, "Connie, are you sure you're gay?"

"I've never loved anyone like I love Kasey. I am whatever that makes me." She looked directly at him. "I like your directness, Tom. Tell me, is there something I'm supposed to be doing? Do I need to make it obvious that I'm gay?"

"No. You have the same choice Michael and I have. We've been together almost twelve years, and we live a very private life. There are only a few straight people who actually know we're gay. We don't make our lifestyle obvious. We can let them know, or not. You have to keep in mind, though, that two people of the same sex living together in their tweener years become obvious anyway."

"What do you mean by *tweener* years?"

"Society accepts college-aged people and old people, especially women, living together. During the years in between, though, it's looked upon with suspicion. Even if no one says it to your face, they're talking at home. Think about how many people you come in contact with on a regular basis: family, neighbors, coworkers, bank clerks, waitresses, mail carriers. They'll figure it out after seeing you together over a period of time. Many times it comes down to personality. If they like you, it's not an issue. A member of the opposite sex, though, attracted and curious, can pose a whole different set of problems. And you're inevitably going to come across those." He paused, realizing the load he had given her. "It wasn't my intent to discourage you, Connie."

"You haven't. I've never let being a woman be a handicap, or its challenges scare me. I chose a career in a predominantly male field. I've dealt with condescension and sexism. Being gay doesn't scare me. The thought of losing Kasey does."

"Is there something I can do to help?"

131

"What do you think Kasey needs from me right now?"

Tom thought for a moment. "Maybe a show of strength on your part. If you could somehow show her the strength of your love."

"You think I should go to her?"

"If I were in your place, that's exactly what I'd do." He took her hand. "If I were you, wherever she was weak, I'd try to be strong. Wherever she was unsure, I'd be sure. And look for your chance to show her how much you love her."

Connie stood and picked up her keys, anxious now to get things in motion. "Thank you, Tom. You don't know how much of a relief this has been." She gave him a thankful hug. "I've felt so helpless."

"I love Kasey like a sister. If you're going to be good for her, there isn't anything I'd like better than to see you two together."

TWENTY-TWO

The sun radiated its heat from the worn old wood of the raft. Kasey spread her towel and welcomed its comfort. She rested her chin on folded arms and surveyed her lake. A fresh gentle breeze chased mischievously through leaves of maple and oak and teased the calmest water into playful nudges of the old raft. She was at home here. It was her life's only constant, and her only true solace. It had hidden her when Cindy left and comforted her memories when her mother died. It was something she could always count on, a place she would never give up. Here, mind speaks to the soul uninterrupted; cries of the heart find the length and breadth needed to be free. And here, without scrutiny, half-truths are made whole.

She would do it alone. She always had. She would sift the final grains of sand and balance the weight of emotion and logic. She would come to a place that her soul could tolerate and find peace for her heart. Here, at last, mind and soul could come face to face, and held in the balance was the love of Connie Bradford.

It wasn't doubt of Connie's love that drove Kasey from her arms. Rather, it was temperance. Without the test of heat, no metal proves its strength; without the test of life, no love can prove its worth. Rare is the love that survives the tests of the life she knew, but the pain from loves that failed those tests could fill more than one lifetime.

Within this lifetime, though, was an interlude that had brought a smile from deep in her heart, that had made her happier than she could ever remember. For that little while, life had become an adventure again, and for the first time in a long while Kasey Hollander had begun to feel once more.

At the sound of a motor, Kasey raised her head and looked toward shore. Through sun-spotted eyes she strained to see whose car had stopped beside the cabin. *Dammit, Sharon. You've made yourself clear. I need to do this alone.*

But it wasn't the squareness of Sharon's shape that emerged from the sun's glare. Kasey waited until Connie reached the end of the dock. "What are you doing here?"

"You can't hide from this forever," she called back. "We have to talk about it."

"Talking's not going to fix it. Go home, Connie." *Get back in the car. Take your curiosity and your temptation of love and go home. Maybe I can never get over you, but I'm sure as hell going to try.* Connie remained, hands on her hips, staring out at the raft. Kasey watched, unmoving.

"You're not coming in?" Connie asked finally.

"No."

Without another word, Connie took off her shoes, her watch, and her sunglasses. At first, Kasey didn't realize what she was watching. Then she sat straight up. Before she could say anything, Connie dove in fully clothed and began swimming to the raft. "And I thought *I* was crazy."

Connie pulled herself up the ladder, shirt clinging tightly to her breasts. A resistant Kasey pulled her eyes away and handed her the towel. There wasn't a lesbian she knew who would still be saying no at this point. Sage Bristo would be helping her out of her wet clothes by now and warming her in a heated embrace. Connie dried her face and hair.

"So what is going to fix it?" she asked breathlessly.

"I don't know, Connie."

"Kasey, if you can look into my eyes" — she made eye contact and hesitated, still breathless — "and tell me you don't feel what I feel, then I'll leave right now."

Kasey's eyes widened in realization, deepened with honesty. "I do feel the same thing, Connie. That's the problem. That wasn't a friendship kiss we had, and it's why we left the club early."

Although her heart jumped with excitement at Kasey's admission, Connie held her emotions in check. "I don't understand why it's a problem if we both feel the same way."

Looking out into the water, Kasey said softly, "I won't make it through another situation like I had with Cindy. It'll destroy me."

"Honey, look at me." Kasey's eyes came quickly to her. "I'm not Cindy. Don't you think I'm strong enough to be gay?"

"I've been this way all my life."

With a gentle smile she offered, "I'm a quick study."

Kasey smiled as she looked out into the water.

Connie watched her and waited. The fear Kasey was

struggling against must be enormous. She could only hope the love she felt was enough. "Are you strong enough to love me?"

Kasey had not expected this insight, true to its mark. Connie had seen what she couldn't — that she wasn't even judging Connie by Cindy's fears but was judging her by Kasey Hollander's fears. And beyond those fears, lay Connie's love and pain. Indeed she wasn't Cindy. Connie Bradford, insightful and decisive, knew exactly what she wanted. And she had the courage to face the unknown for it. It was embarrassing not to be able to say the same of herself.

Kasey stood, then paused as she looked down into Connie's uplifted face. "I love you so much it scares me," she said, then dove into the water.

The relief was greater than any Connie had ever felt, with the exception of the moment her mother had opened her eyes in the hospital. Connie watched Kasey's powerful strokes slice through the water until she reached the dock. Her words had created an excitement that removed all the worry of the past week. But still she resisted the impulse to follow after her. She wanted a little time to absorb it all. It wasn't hard to imagine what would happen now. They would give themselves to each other, soothe each other's fears, explore the mystery together. They would be lovers.

Minutes later, she slipped back into the chilling water and swam to the dock.

Kasey watched from the doorway of the cabin. The sight made her smile. The woman she loved was trudging across the little yard, shoes in hand, clothes holding fast to the lines and curves of an admirable figure. How could she have even considered shutting her out of her life? How could she have consciously put them both through certain heartache for fear of what may never happen? She knew now, she could never have done that.

"Do you always swim with your clothes on?" she asked, watching Connie come up the porch steps.

"Only on special occasions."

"Why don't you take them off and hang them over the railing. I've got a towel and dry clothes for you." She watched in amusement as Connie struggled out of everything except her underwear. As she came in the door, Kasey wrapped the towel and her arms around her.

"It's amazing what a woman has to go through to get you to hold her." Connie wrapped her arms around Kasey's waist.

"You do know that there are a lot of lesbians out there that aren't this weird."

"Uh-huh. But I'm only concerned with one."

"Yes, and you picked the most heterophobic one on the block."

She pulled back to look into Kasey's eyes, heart pounding uncontrollably. "I've had quite a lot to figure out and understand over the past four months. It hasn't been easy. But except for Mom being sick, I wouldn't trade one minute of it."

"Neither would I," admitted Kasey, pulling Connie close again and holding her gently.

Kasey's embrace, warm and strong, felt so right. The dampness of Connie's skin warmed quickly to her touch. She pressed her cheek against her hair and breathed in her scent until their closeness began to do more than chase away the chill of the lake.

"I've been so afraid of wanting you," Kasey whispered, stroking Connie's wet, shiny hair.

"And I've been afraid you didn't."

"God. If you only knew," Kasey said, as Connie's arms tightened into a firm, full embrace.

"I think I'm about to," she said, stepping from their embrace. "But not before I shower. Don't go anywhere."

"I put clean clothes in the bathroom," Kasey smiled. "I'll put a fire on."

"You've already done that."

With the sun going down and the wind from the lake chilling the little cabin, the warmth from the fire felt wonderful. Kasey leaned back against the pulled out couch, her arms folded around her bare knees, and stared into the leaping flames. Apprehension had given way to anticipation. Twinges of excitement began finding their way into her consciousness. Things were changing. No more repressing. No more denying. Connie excited her. She made her happy. Kasey's heart was about to win the battle. And from now on her mind would be taking lessons from her heart.

Connie slipped onto the end of the bed behind Kasey. Her fingers traced through her soft golden hair before coming to rest on Kasey's shoulder. "What is it that makes a fire so sensual?"

"The ambiance it throws over everything. It makes everything look so warm." She knew Connie's eyes were not focused on the flames. They were concentrating instead on the glow the flames cast on Kasey's face, in her eyes. Connie's hand gently stroked the firm smoothness of Kasey's arm, then moved beneath the sleeve of her T-shirt. The heat erupting in Kasey's body rivaled the effects of the logs flaming before them. Her heart pounded with anticipation.

With long graceful fingers, Connie reached over and brushed the wispy strands of hair falling across Kasey's forehead. Her index finger traced lightly down the pretty profile. Kasey smiled and kissed the tip of it when it touched her lips.

"Hey, pretty eyes," Connie said softly. "What are you thinking?"

Kasey took Connie's hand and held it to her face. As she on the bed, she looked up into Connie's eyes. "About how much I've missed you all week. I've been awful to work with."

"So have I. I'm glad to know it had the same effect on you." Her eyes wandered lovingly over Kasey's face before settling on her lips.

Softly Kasey warned, "Don't look at me like that unless you mean it."

"Oh, I mean it," she whispered back, her eyes fixed on Kasey's.

Kasey's eyes moved to Connie's beautiful lips, her heart racing. Softly she whispered, "Tell me what you want."

"I want you to kiss me again. And this time don't stop."

Warm, slow touches of her wonderful lips awakened the ache that had started a long week ago. They tasted each other, open and wet. A low moan told of Connie's pleasure, expressing passion never experienced with a man. Kasey pulled her lips from Connie's. Teasingly delicate touches from the tip of her tongue sent a current from Connie's lips to her very center. Her eyes opened into the blue intensity enveloping her. "Yes," was all she said, short and whispery, an expression of the beginning fire of passion. Connie pressed her open mouth to Kasey and yielded to the softness.

She grabbed Kasey's T-shirt in a silent demand for closeness. Kasey climbed onto the bed, pressed warm kisses into her neck, and gathered Connie into her arms. Their bodies, defined beneath their T-shirts by the heat they were creating, now pressed into a full embrace. They explored carefully with their hands, their mouths, their eyes. Gently nuzzling and caressing.

"This is wonderful," murmured Connie. "I never knew it could be like this." The slowness of their caresses nurtured not only their physical desire for each other but also a special span of time that had always been missing for

Connie — a time that provided a tenderness she needed, a slowness, a crescendo of emotion. And while their eyes spoke love to each other, their physical excitement grew to an overwhelming tension.

"How do you make me ache so?" Connie whispered. "Never have I wanted anyone like this."

Kasey met her lips again, the excitement of love and passion surging through her. She kissed Connie deeply, wanted her desperately. Her hands found the warmth of Connie's skin beneath the loose shirt and covered her with loving touches. Sighs of appreciation became gasps of pleasure at the gentle squeezing of a hardened nipple, at teasing fingers slipping around the waistband of her panties.

Connie's hands also explored — over the nicely muscled thighs, over the round firm buttocks, under cloth to feel the strength of her back. "Take this off, Kasey," she whispered, pushing the shirt up.

Kasey removed her T-shirt and underwear while the fire's red glow danced among the golden hairs and flickered across her beautiful form. There was no nervousness, no apprehension; there was only appreciation and love as Connie reached for Kasey. Her expressive hands glided freely over the warm, smooth skin. No one would ever be able to convince her now that this was wrong. Nothing this deep in her soul could ever be denied. She was sure of that now, very, very sure. She closed her arms, embracing Kasey's strong naked body. Tantalizing touches from her lips whispered across Kasey's shoulder and up the back of her neck. Her hands covered the soft breasts, firm rosebuds pressing into her palms. Releasing a deep slow breath, Kasey leaned her head back submissively. "You're absolutely beautiful," whispered Connie, squeezing the buds between her fingers.

In the dimness Connie caught a brief glimpse of shimmering blue lifting from her body to look into her eyes. "I've wanted to be skin to skin with you from the first time

I saw you." Kasey's words filled Connie with excitement as Kasey's arms laid her gently back on the bed. Strong hands touched her, softly and carefully. Caressing, touching, loving her. And her body answered them, moving to them, wanting their caring, needing their arousal. Connie surrendered to their tenderness until her whole being belonged to her new lover.

For the first time in her life, someone was making love to her, pleasing her, giving unselfishly to her. She didn't think it was possible to be any more in love with Kasey, but her love seemed to be growing with each new whisper, each new sensation. She closed her eyes and savored every touch as Kasey's wonderful lips kissed her breasts, her neck. Connie's body moved to her lover's fervor and asked for more. Part of her wanted the sensations to go on forever; another part of her wanted this need driven to its climax. Never before had she relinquished control like this. Never before had she trusted so completely. Connie opened her eyes as Kasey moved her warm naked body up against her. There wasn't an experience in her life that compared with the sensuousness of this woman's body against her own. Hot wetness sliding together, the heat of her melting into Kasey, no longer separate. "I love you so much, Connie."

Connie tasted the sweet skin, breathing in the scent of her. "You're everything I've ever dreamed of," she whispered. She felt the heat of Kasey's desire for her and gave in to an intensity that rocked her body with sensation. Desire now electrified every nerve, clouded thought, demanded satisfaction. She rode desperately the thigh pressed between her legs. She cried out her desperation on ragged breaths, until finally a hand slid under her buttocks, cradling her gently. The other hand replaced Kasey's thigh, and her strong skillful fingers stroked Connie wonderfully and perfectly, creating a feeling of desire so incredible that Connie could no longer tell which hand was doing what. "Oh, yes, Kasey, yes," she gasped, "I love you...I...

love you." She had no control left. It was lost completely to the accomplished hands and the warm wet mouth on her breast. With a tremendous cry of release she came to her lover in a strong and powerful orgasm — the first not of her own making. She had come so easily, as easily as she had fallen in love with Kasey, as intensely as she had always known it should be.

For the next few minutes she enjoyed being nestled in Kasey's embrace, her body still tingling with pleasure. She welcomed the sweet kisses and delicate touch of Kasey's fingertips as they traced imaginary lines along the contours of her body.

"I don't think you'll ever know how much I love you," Connie said, following Kasey's eyes up to her own.

"How long do you think it will take to show me?"

"I'd say at least a lifetime."

"Then maybe you'd better start right now," Kasey said softly. She lay back on the bed, pulling Connie with her.

"You're such a wonderful lover." She gently stroked Kasey's face. "I don't know if I can —"

"Shh," she whispered. "You will."

Carefully, almost reverently, Connie caressed and kissed the smooth, taut skin of Kasey's body. She realized very soon how wonderful it was to feel the woman she loved responding to her touch, moving to her rhythm, and wanting her lips, her tongue, her love. And almost too soon Connie knew the joy of satisfying a woman. She felt the power of the orgasm she had created and drew excitement from it as she drew air into her lungs. It exhilarated her with a thrill nearing the emotional ecstasy of her own orgasm. But the emotion of it went on, past desire, past orgasm. She couldn't stop. There was so much more she needed to give. She continued to cover Kasey's breasts and neck and lips with kisses filled with feelings of love.

"Mmm, you're so very good," Kasey managed between kisses. "Have you ever given this much love before?"

Nuzzling her face into Kasey's neck, she answered, "I've never felt this kind of love before. How did you do this to me?"

"I don't know, but I'm glad I did."

For some time after, they talked and cuddled and narrowed their world to each other. They looked into each other's heart and found themselves there. It was the closeness Connie had always longed for, a closeness she never wanted to be without again. Kasey pulled the blanket over Connie and got up. "I'll be right back." Snuggling beneath the blanket, Connie watched her lover's outline dimly lit against the darkness as she approached the fireplace.

The white ashes, still in the shape of a log, began falling away, exposing the red coals within. Kasey knelt and stirred the fading coals before adding fresh wood. A soft, warm glow momentarily illuminated her face before she disappeared into the shadows. For a strange moment she seemed like a vision in a dream, one that had always just eluded her awakened thought. Now, though, her vision had a face, a name, and a love for her that she could feel.

The stirred coals flickered again with renewed life. As Kasey slipped in under the blanket, the small flames grew stronger and hotter, quietly spreading their warmth. With the feel of Kasey's skin against hers, Connie closed her eyes and whispered, "Make love to me again, so I know you're not a dream."

Finally consumed by the heat, the logs burst into flames, lighting up the little room. Its warmth would last until dawn.

TWENTY-THREE

Neither of them had wanted to leave the cabin yesterday, and neither of them had wanted to part last night. Both, however, needed to prepare for work this morning, and benefited from a full night's sleep. Kasey leaped up the front steps of the porch. Sharon and Troy were already at work, but nothing was going to bother her today. Not the traffic, not being late, not even Sharon. Not today. She felt wonderful. Today, the house could fall down around her and she'd patiently put it back together, piece by piece. She smiled to herself.

From the entranceway she could see Sharon diligently

applying mud to a joint on the dining room wall. Quietly, Kasey crept up behind her and grabbed her sides, startling Sharon so much she dropped the mud knife.

"Dammit, Kasey!" she yelled, slightly embarrassed at her sudden fright.

Kasey grabbed her around the shoulders. She hugged her as she laughed and kissed the side of her head. "I'm sorry," she apologized with a big smile.

Sharon picked up the knife and scraped the mud off the floor. "I guess I don't have to ask what this mood means," she said with detectable sarcasm. "I figured as much after the first hour and you still weren't here."

"That part you're wrong about," returned Kasey on her way out of the room. "I went to the county building and picked up the deed for this place. I have to drop it off at the bank today. Otherwise," she said, sticking her head back around the corner of the doorway, "you're right."

Sharon shook her head as she watched her friend disappear into the hallway. Knowing all too well how strong the impulses of love are, she had expected the situation to evolve as it had, sooner or later. Yet as happy as it seemed to make Kasey, Sharon wasn't pleased at all. *Just another heartache waiting to happen,* she thought, as she went back to work.

Entering the kitchen that had frustrated her so last week, Kasey leaned over a kneeling Troy and wrapped her arms around his neck. "Hey, handsome," she said, kissing his cheek.

"Hey, yourself," he said as he stood. "You must have had a great weekend. You haven't acted like this since —"

"Never mind. You ready to send this thing into the driveway?" She motioned toward the sink and counter.

"Whatever your heart desires," he grinned.

"It'll have to do for now."

"Let's do it," he said, handing her the crowbar.

They worked hard through the rest of the morning,

tearing out the old plumbing and sink and clearing the kitchen of the old cabinets in good time to break for lunch. "Nice work, Stanley," Kasey remarked, watching Troy load the last of the rotted flooring into the construction bin.

"Why, thank you, Ollie," he teased back, characteristically scratching the top of his head.

"Time for lunch, wouldn't you say?" she asked, picking up the tools from the floor.

"That would be wonderful, Ollie."

An unexpected knock directed their attention toward the side door where Connie stood in the doorway holding a dozen long-stemmed roses. "How's my timing?" she asked, with a captivating smile. "Is it soup yet?"

"Hey, Connie, those for me?" Troy teased.

"This one is." She took one de-thorned rose and laid it over his ear. "And these are for you," she said, walking toward Kasey.

"Ooh, it *must* have been a good weekend," Troy beamed.

"Bye, Troy," Kasey said, not taking her eyes from Connie's. "Shut the door on your way out."

He headed for the doorway, still smiling. "There isn't one." Then turning around he added, "Don't forget that."

Kasey, however, wrapped up in the moment, wasn't thinking about anything except Connie.

In the years that he had known Kasey was gay, Troy had never seen her show that kind of affection toward another woman. He hesitated only long enough to see the beginning of a very passionate embrace. Neither had he ever seen two women kiss each other, only motherly and sisterly kisses. From the things he had heard from other guys and things he had read, he was supposed to be either disgusted, or turned on by it. Funny, he thought, walking down the hall, he was neither. Although he could clearly see their desire for each other, it didn't excite him sexually, and it definitely didn't disgust him. Maybe it was because of how much he cared for Kasey and that he really liked Connie; or maybe it was because he had grown up with Kasey's influence. But for whatever reason, seeing them together like that just made him happy.

Sharon was cleaning up her tools when Troy appeared in the doorway. "You ready for lunch?"

"Close. How about Kasey?"

"She's not coming. Connie's here."

"What the hell is that?" Sharon asked, looking at the rose behind his ear.

He just smiled and stuck the rose in his tool pouch and hung it on the door knob.

"Don't tell me she brought her flowers."

"Sure did," he said with a big smile.

She rolled her eyes. "Let's get out of here before I lose my appetite."

"You should give her a chance," Troy returned, following her out the door.

Obviously not in agreement, Sharon kept on walking and ignored the comment. He knew better than to press the subject further.

The mood, of course, was much different in the kitchen. With their kisses becoming much too intense for the situation and Connie's hips beginning to create desire that couldn't be satisfied during a lunch break, Kasey pulled back. "If you keep that up, neither of us is going back to work today."

Smiling, Connie replied, "I love how you make me feel. I'll be thinking about you all day."

"Too bad you can't take an executive lunch; we could go to my house for the afternoon."

She nuzzled Kasey's neck. "Mmm, don't tempt me. If it weren't for end of the month reports . . ."

Between soft kisses to Connie's face and neck, Kasey whispered, "I love you."

Connie looked into the eyes that had touched her heart

from the very first day. "And I love you — more than anything."

Unable to resist the torrent of heat flooding her body, Kasey kissed her with such intensity they lost all sense of time. Connie's hands explored beneath Kasey's old worn T-shirt, and Kasey pulled Connie's trim hips tightly into the heat of her body. Time lost relevance as seemingly nothing existed beyond their desire for each other. So much love needed expressing.

Connie closed her eyes. A soft moan escaped her lips as Kasey's mouth ravished the tender skin of her neck and chest. Buttons opened quickly, and in an instant Connie was pressing the swell of her breast through the thin material of her bra into the heat of Kasey's mouth. "Ohhh, I want you," she whispered, tenderly grasping Kasey's earlobe between her teeth. "Right here — right now."

She felt Kasey's hands find the closure of her slacks just as the loud slam of the front door suddenly shocked them back to reality.

"Hey, Kase?" Troy yelled, as they released their embrace. "Can I come in?"

"Uh . . ."

Connie hurriedly rebuttoned her blouse.

"Yeah," Kasey called back.

Troy walked through the doorway with a big grin and a large fast-food bag. "I brought you guys some lunch," he said, with a hint of shyness.

Subconsciously Connie ran her fingers over the buttons in a final check. "Thank you, Troy."

"You're a sweetheart," Kasey added.

"Yeah, I know, with a minor operation," he teased, handing the bag to Kasey.

Connie looked puzzled. "What?"

"It's an inside joke, I'll explain it later."

Suddenly Connie glanced at her watch. "Ooh, I have ten minutes to get back. I'll have to eat this on the way.

Thanks, Troy, that was very thoughtful." She redirected her attention to Kasey. "Come to my house tonight?"

Kasey nodded. She formed the words *I love you* silently as Connie backed out the side door, the glint of a new lover in her eyes.

"Sorry if I interrupted anything," Troy apologized.

"It's a good thing you did. We weren't keeping track of time very well."

He watched Kasey delve into her fries. "Kase, would you mind if I asked you something personal?"

"Maybe. It depends on what it is."

"I just wondered if you two were officially together now."

The tone of her voice was thoughtful. "I think you can safely say that."

"I'm glad. I really like Connie. But mostly, I like how happy she makes you."

Kasey looked adoringly at her cousin. "You know, I can't remember the last time I told you how much I appreciate you. You're very special. And you're going to make some woman a wonderful partner."

His focus never left the floor. "You've told me lots of times, Kase."

"Guess I've embarrassed you enough today then," she said, handing him the tape measure and grabbing her sandwich at the same time. "Let's get back to work."

TWENTY-FOUR

Days of happiness had turned into weeks of cohabited bliss. Whether at Kasey's house or Connie's, their non-working time was spent exclusively together. Life, it seemed, was wonderful.

"Wow, the porch looks great," declared Connie, coming across the yard.

"Your timing's perfect. We just finished, except for one last check." Kasey set the level across the top step. "Anyone looking?" she asked.

"You're as bad as your ol' man," grinned Troy.

Kasey only laughed and knocked her knuckles once on

the step in front of the level where the bubble rested perfectly between the lines.

"Is this another inside joke?"

"Sort of," replied Troy. "Her dad always asks that when he's finished a difficult job and he's making the final check to see if a piece fits or if it's level. Then when you say something stupid like 'Just me, why?' he says, 'Cuz I'm about to walk on water.' "

"Pretty sure of himself, isn't he?" Connie laughed.

"If I hadn't been watching him, I would've sworn he'd already checked it. He's a character, but he's good."

"He has his moments," returned Kasey.

"You must have inherited some of them," Connie said. "That looks pretty level to me."

"So now you're a quick-study carpenter's assistant, I suppose," laughed Kasey.

"Maybe the city will hire her as an inspector," Troy chimed in. "Then we wouldn't have to put up with ol' whats-his-breath."

"Larry Lush? He's 80 proof by nine A.M. Yep," agreed Kasey. "I definitely think you ought to apply."

"Would I have to put up with characters like you two all day long?"

Troy shook his head, "Worse."

"Never mind, I'll keep my day job. Which reminds me, I have to get back. I just stopped to tell you to be ready to leave your house at six-thirty, Kase. I've got reservations for seven."

"You're still not going to tell me where we're going?"

"No, it's part of your birthday surprise. All I'll tell you is, don't eat lunch and dress to the nines, as my grandma used to say."

"Any special requests on what I should wear?"

"Anything, so long as I can see lots of leg, and don't cover your arms."

Troy nudged his cousin playfully. "A little skin, Kase."

"What do you want me to wear?" Connie asked.

"You know what I like," Kasey said with a tilt of her head.

"Yes, but we're going to be in public," she returned with a not-so-innocent smile. "Sorry, Troy. The peach dress, right?"

Kasey nodded with a smile and watched Connie back across the yard.

"Don't let her be late, Troy," she called from the drive. "And don't forget that we're stopping at Sharon's for a drink after."

Kasey nodded and waved as the car backed out of the drive.

"You're voluntarily taking Connie to face Attila the Hun?"

She shook her head. "I'm sure it's a mistake. We even argued over it, and Connie's the one insisting on going."

"Why?"

"Connie thinks that if we don't go, Sharon will assume that Connie was the one who didn't want to, and that will give Sharon one more reason to dislike her. Connie's really trying to make Sharon give her a chance. The bottom line is, she doesn't want to affect my relationship with Sharon."

"Not possible."

"You and I know that, but Connie is an incredible optimist."

"Man, she's nothin' like Cindy."

"One more reason why I love her so much, and probably why I gave in," admitted Kasey. "I was up front with Sharon, though. I made her promise to behave or I wouldn't come."

Troy cocked his head. "But you know Attila," he chuckled. "No prisoners."

"Connie's not easily intimidated. Then again, I'm sure she's never run through the bramble bushes bare legged.

It's a shame to ruin what I'm sure will be an otherwise wonderful evening. But I've got to give Connie a chance, too."

"Happy birthday anyway," he said, giving Kasey a quick hug on his way up the steps.

TWENTY-FIVE

Keeping her secret right to the last minute, Connie pulled into the crowded parking lot of a large, beautifully lighted restaurant. "The South Sea?" Kasey remarked, reading the tropical looking neon sign.

"Have you ever been here?"

"No, but it looks interesting."

"According to Tom, this is supposed to be *the* Polynesian restaurant."

A parking valet met them at the entrance. Connie snapped off her car ring and handed it to him. She smiled excitedly as Kasey came around the car. "Well, let's see," she said as they entered through a huge wooden door. They were greeted quickly by a man adorned in colorful ethnic attire and directed across a bridge that spanned an actual stream. Entering the main part of the restaurant, both women were immediately struck by its magnitude and beauty. Narrow paths wound around plots of tropical plants that nestled privately among splashes of brilliant flowers. And stretching magnificently the full three stories along the back wall was a man-made cliff side.

As they began their ascent along the paths to the next level they could see a body of soft blue water, surrounded by large rocks, that rested directly below the cliff wall. "Unbelievable," exclaimed Kasey.

"He said it was like a little piece of paradise. Wait 'til you see where we're sitting."

They continued across bridges and up the path to a table by itself right next to the cliff. From their vantage point the water below was in full view and few other tables were visible. An excellent use of elevation, rocks and foliage provided privacy and a maximum view of the artificially created paradise. It was truly a remarkable artistic achievement. "This is absolutely gorgeous," proclaimed Kasey.

"If the food is as good as the atmosphere, we are in paradise."

Immediately after the waiter brought their drinks, Connie noticed two women dressed in brightly colored bathing suits making their way along the rocks overlooking the water.

Kasey turned to see what she was watching. "What are they doing?"

"You'll see."

One woman stopped on a flat rock just above the water while the other continued climbing the cliff to a ledge directly across from their table. Although Connie knew what was happening, she too was witnessing it for the first time. She looked down at the distance separating the ledge from the water. It was frightening.

"She's not going to dive from there, is she?" Kasey asked with guarded excitement.

"Just watch."

The dark, beautifully muscled woman readied herself. Then suddenly, with arms spread wide, she pushed fearlessly into the air. Silently, in complete awe, they watched the lovely form effortlessly complete a perfect dive into the water below. "Wow!" exclaimed Kasey.

"That was unbelievable."

"It was breathtaking," Kasey said, her eyes still riveted on the ripples of blue so far below.

The diver emerged from the surface to a resounding applause echoing from every part of the building. She held something up in her hand, pulled herself from the water, and handed it to the woman on the rock.

"She got something from the bottom. Did you see that? What do you think it is?" She looked over at the smile on Connie's face. "You already know." Her eyes darted back to the woman now making her way around the edge of the water.

Joy radiated from Connie's face. To see the pleasure that tonight brought her lover made her gift all she had hoped it would be. She watched with delight while Kasey watched the woman with the long dark hair continue up the path. She carried a lei of bright fuchsia flowers and offered a bright white smile as she approached and placed the lei around Kasey's neck. "Happy Birthday," she said with a kiss to her cheek. The look on Kasey's face was priceless. Her eyes filled with childlike wonder and surprise, and her cheeks flushed as she watched in silence. Then the woman presented still another gift. With swift mastery, she opened the large clam she had carried from the diver and stole the treasure from within.

With a discerning smile, Kasey met Connie's twinkling eyes. "A pearl."

"A nice large one," the woman remarked.

"It's beautiful," she said, examining her treasure. "Thank you."

First in her native tongue, then in English, the woman said, "It is hoped that this day brings you warm winds and a calm sea, and love to fill your heart."

"Thank you," Kasey smiled, finding Connie's eyes. "It has."

They turned and waved their thank you to the diver watching from the rocks below and received a pretty smile in return.

Kasey turned back to Connie's happy eyes and whispered, "I wish I could kiss you right now. What a beautiful birthday this is."

Connie reached across the table and took Kasey's hand. "I love you, Kasey, with all my heart."

It was a shame that as much as she wanted to enjoy this moment, in all its wonder and romanticism, Kasey was unable to prevent their surroundings from creeping into her peripheral vision. Years of perpetual paranoia had set their tabs, and despite efforts to ignore them this time, she could not. The man in her peripheral had been watching their every move intently. Discreetly, she slipped her hand from Connie's and replaced it with the pearl.

Throughout dinner the man continued his vigil. His wife even moved her chair to see what was so interesting to her husband. Connie continued unaware, which Kasey found unusually refreshing. She felt almost righteous in denying him his effect. She decided to enjoy the feeling for as long as it lasted, probably until Connie noticed him.

Only minutes later, as they waited for dessert and spoke of exotic plants, Connie did notice. "How long have they been watching us?"

"Off and on," replied Kasey, playing down its significance.

"Does it bother you?"

"No. I guess it's kind of a compliment to be more interesting than all this." She let her eyes sweep around them, but purposely avoided his stare.

Once again Connie reached over and took Kasey's hand. "Let's do anniversaries here," she said. "That way if we're ever confused as to how many years we've been together, we can count pearls."

Kasey picked a flower from her lei and slid it into the shiny dark hair over Connie's ear. Delicate rose-purple petals intensified the brilliant deep blue of the eyes twinkling their message of love. "You never cease to amaze me, Connie Bradford," she smiled. "I am so in love with you."

As they left the restaurant and passed the table of the couple who had so curiously watched them all evening, the man made his judgment known. "What a horrible waste."

Kasey avoided his eyes, while Connie offered the couple her most professional smile. "Good night," she said graciously.

Waste? Kasey thought. *Waste is the time it would take to try to change such malevolent thinking.* She conceded, however, that it was important that such ignorance not be allowed to foster anger, a thought with which Connie Bradford evidently agreed.

TWENTY-SIX

Connie brought the car to a stop on the nearly deserted street in front of Sharon's house. Kasey tried again. "Honey, it's been such a beautiful evening. We don't have to stop. I'll call her when we get home and tell her we were too tired."

"Yes, it has been a wonderful evening, and there's no reason to think this is going to spoil it. Besides, how would that make you feel if you were Sharon?"

"Then promise me we won't stay long, okay?"

"Agreed. But before we go in, I want to give you your present." She reached for a small box behind the seat.

"Connie, tonight's been enough of a present..."

"Open."

Kasey stared for a moment into Connie's loving eyes, then leaned over and kissed her.

"You haven't even seen it yet," she smiled.

"I don't have to, to know how I feel." Kasey's voice was low and soft. "Are you sure you don't want to go home?"

With a gentle laugh Connie replied, "Open it."

The box contained a wide, gold herringbone necklace matching the bracelet Kasey always wore. "Oh, Connie, I know how much these are. I've never been able to afford one. Why did you spend so much?" she asked, admiring her gift.

"I got a special deal. Besides, you're worth it."

"A special payment plan, I'm sure."

"Here, put it on. I want to see how it looks," she said, leaning over to fasten the clasp. "There. Perfect."

"Didn't we do this once before?"

"We sure did, but this time I don't think you're going to run from me," she said, pressing her lips to Kasey's. The kiss quickly began to express hours of suppressed emotion. Then just as quickly, Connie pulled away. "Nope, nope, we've got to stop this. We are going to see Sharon."

With a smile Kasey opened the door. "Don your armor. Here we go."

"Whose car is that?" asked Connie.

"Sue's, Sharon's ex. She said Sue and her girlfriend might stop over, too." She rang the doorbell. "They're probably downstairs where it's cool."

After what seemed like an unusually long time, Sharon finally answered the door. "Hi! Well, I was beginning to wonder if you'd make it. Did you have a good time?" Sharon babbled. "You look great."

"Yes, we had a wonderful time. You should see this restaurant . . ." Kasey began, walking through the living room.

"Okay, finish telling me downstairs. I've got to run to the bathroom first."

Kasey took Connie's hand and started down the lighted stairway. But partway down she said, "That's weird. The basement light's not on."

"Where's the switch?"

"At the bottom here." Kasey reached for the switch.

Suddenly they were startled by a loud wolf whistle and a deafening "Happy Birthday" as light flooded the basement. They stood astounded, facing a crowd of laughing, cheering people. The look on Kasey's face must have told the story.

"We got you! We got you!" Sue exclaimed. "You didn't know, did you?"

Kasey shook her head in complete surprise, then turned to Connie. "You knew, didn't you?"

Connie shook her head.

"She didn't know," confirmed Sharon from behind. "Come on, see who all is here. Make yourself comfortable. That is, if you can in those clothes."

Connie tried not to be overwhelmed as Kasey guided her through the crowd with greetings and introductions. She was grateful when they finally reached the other side of the room and found Tom. She was much more at ease as they shared the restaurant experience with him.

Another couple soon joined their little group. Kasey introduced the women as friends she had known for most of their eleven years together. Evonne, round and matronly, with mostly graying curls and a smile that would melt ice, looked to be in her fifties. Donna, robust and ruddy, looking very much like a grown-up Huck Finn, was probably in her early forties.

Their natural warmth and comfortable conversation

offered Connie an acceptance she sensed almost immediately. She listened with an appreciative smile, realizing immediately how much Kasey admired and respected these two women and how much *she* already liked them.

"Do you like horses, Connie?" Evonne asked.

"Yes, but I haven't been around them much since high school."

"We have two beautiful horses that need to be ridden more often. You'll have to get Kasey to bring you out riding some day soon." Evonne redirected her attention. "Kasey, you haven't been out to ride for some time."

"I know. I've had so much going on lately. We will, though, maybe next weekend —"

"Will you look at *that*?" Donna said, suddenly grabbing Evonne's arm. She was directing her attention to the bottom of the stairs where a tall, voluptuous blond stood next to Michael. The sequined gown twinkled reflected colors as she moved toward the only light, over the platform.

"Now I remember," smiled Kasey.

"I can't imagine you forgetting someone who looked like that," Donna teased.

"No," exclaimed Kasey. "That's Randy."

The women, fascinated by the revelation, stared at the figure standing at the microphone. Leaning close to Kasey, Connie whispered, "That's the man Tom introduced us to?"

Kasey nodded and smiled.

"That's amazing," remarked Connie. "How does he do that?"

"Lots of little tricks," returned Kasey, rolling her eyes at the unintentional pun.

Randy's soft, sultry voice sounded over the microphone. "Kasey, come up here, dear. This is for you."

She made her way across the room, Connie in hand, just as Tom emerged from the stairway with a large cake. He motioned for Kasey to change places with him.

Thirty-six lighted candles flickered a taunting glow. "You put every one of them on here, too, didn't you? Thanks so much, Tom."

"But you're such a beautiful old lady," he laughed.

As Kasey stood conspicuously behind the lighted confection, Randy, in his breathless falsetto, offered his version of the famous Marilyn birthday song.

Meanwhile, Connie was still finding it difficult to visualize a man before her. It didn't seem possible. The movements were ultrafeminine. The voice was even believable. She took Tom's arm. "Does he do this professionally?"

"He's a female impersonator," he said with a big smile. "I'm afraid Sharon has enrolled you in a crash course in gay socialization."

"You might want to find a seat for this," announced Randy, as the applause faded. "Kasey, we didn't want you to feel out of place all dressed up. So as you're going to see, I'm not the only one in drag. Tonight, for your entertainment delight we present" — his outstretched hand directed their attention to the stairway where three women dressed in evening gowns made their way unsteadily toward the platform — "The Sappho Sisters."

"How do hets walk in these damn things," the last one was saying.

"Extra chromosome," said the middle one. "We don't have it."

The first one to the platform, the heavier of the three, looked directly at Kasey. "Baby, I hope you know I shaved my legs just for you."

"Sharon!" Kasey exclaimed in surprise, as she surveyed the thick, square form covered in glittering blue. Connie simply stared in disbelief. "Oooh, baby," Kasey teased, mischievously running her hand up Sharon's leg.

"Behave!" Sharon snapped, slapping her hand. "Damn queer!"

"Oh, but baby, you never looked like this before," laughed Kasey. "You could turn the Orange Queen down the path of perversion."

The entire room was now nearly in tears from laughter, all having figured out by now that the trio of unlikely candidates for homecoming queen consisted of Sharon, Sage, and Jan. Past the initial shock of Sharon's appearance, Kasey's attention shifted to the other two. With wigs hiding their short hair and with their extensive makeup, they were barely recognizable. Only Jan's freckled arms gave her away. Sage was surprisingly the most natural looking with her broad shoulders, narrow hips, and pretty smile.

Still unable to get everyone's attention, Sharon finally called to Tom, "Hit it, maestro," and the trio went into action. "My Guy," altered by Tom's expert handiwork, now talked about "My Girl" while the Sappho Sisters lip-synched their way to fleeting stardom.

"They sure went to a lot of work to do this," remarked Connie.

"This is right up Sharon's alley. She loves this kind of stuff," explained Kasey. "She did surprise me with the dress and makeup, though."

Sharon, meanwhile, hammed it up with first one sister then the other, drawing laughs with her facial expressions and body language. Their funny antics continued through the second verse until suddenly eyes of steel locked onto Connie's. Sharon mouthed the words directly at her, "There's not a man today who could take me away from my girl." How quickly the earlier fun faded, along with Connie's smile. Yet she refused to break eye contact, forcing Sharon to be the one to look away. Somehow it made her feel more in control of the situation. It was such a small thing, happening so quickly that Kasey had missed it altogether. But its impact was undeniable. Its message, loud and clear, was that the rest of the evening may not be as comfortable as the beginning. She decided not to say anything to Kasey.

Sharon spoke over the slowly dying applause, "Do you want to sing a few? Okay, okay. Come on, birthday girl, we need a thorn between these roses." With a smile she held out her hand to Kasey, who pulled up a tight skirt and let Sharon and Sage give her a hand up onto the platform.

"What are we singing?"

"Pretty Woman," came the unison reply.

"This seems to be a tradition around here. Jan?" Kasey signaled.

Grateful for the switch in moods, Connie joined the crowd of happy faces and followed the lead of Kasey's strong voice. But she watched with interest as Kasey interacted with her longtime friend and Sage Bristo. The infamous throaty growl was directed right at Sharon, who returned "Oooh. I love it when you growl dirty." Connie laughed in spite of herself.

The biggest response, though, came from the floor-up once-over Kasey gave Sage and the "mercy" she droned low and slow, an appreciation many obviously shared for the tall, appealing woman from New York. And Sage's smile, directed at Kasey, showed her own appreciation as she slipped her arm comfortably around Kasey's waist. Jealousy was an infrequent visitor to Connie's disposition, but it suddenly made a front-row appearance. She hoped the sexual nuance she was sensing was only the result of a crowd of excited women and her own imagination. The smile she received from Kasey as the song ended was precisely what she needed. She decided there was nothing to worry about.

* * * * *

165

Kasey started off the platform but was stopped by Sharon, who grabbed her arm and the microphone. "Okay, if you want a birthday dance cut in between the short songs on the medley tape," she announced.

"I'm changing first," Sage said.

"Me, too," added Jan, leaving Sharon and Kasey alone on the platform.

"Wusses," muttered Sharon, pulling Kasey into dance position.

"I never thought I'd see this," Kasey grinned, raising an eyebrow at Sharon's dress.

"Don't get used to it. You'll probably never see it again." She kicked off her shoes and began leading to the first song. "And don't step on my feet," she warned.

"Have I ever?"

The women began gathering around the platform, and Connie decided to let Sharon have her fun. Tom and Michael were in the middle of the room wrapped in a slow-moving embrace, so she wound her way between women and chairs and found Evonne and Donna.

"Waiting out the birthday dances?" asked Evonne.

"I don't feel comfortable waiting in line to dance with my lover."

"They're not going to pass up a chance to get the elusive Kasey Hollander in their arms," interjected Donna. "But I don't think it was meant as a personal offense to you, Connie."

"Sharon had this whole thing planned for months," explained Evonne.

"How are you two getting along, by the way?" Donna asked.

"Sharon? I try, but she doesn't like me much."

"Sharon's very protective of Kasey and, don't be

offended by my bluntness, she doesn't like what she thinks are curious straight women," Evonne offered.

"I don't fall into that category, but she sure isn't giving me a chance to prove it."

"She didn't like Evonne either at first," explained Donna. "Evonne was married for a number of years and raised two kids. Now, though, except for Kasey, we're probably her best friends."

"She even stood up with us during our commitment ceremony," added Evonne.

"You're saying there's hope for me yet?" Connie's tone wasn't convincingly optimistic.

"If she doesn't make you hate her first," Evonne grinned. "Time has proven to her that I truly love Donna, and that just because I lived a straight life until then doesn't make me any less a lesbian. Sharon's basically a good person. She's almost too honest, and extremely loyal. Once she's your friend, she's there for life. Try to be patient."

"Are there a lot of others who think like Sharon?"

"I've encountered quite a few. Probably the majority of women here tonight have that attitude to some degree," Evonne answered.

"Does it help if you're out about being gay?"

"I don't know. Keep in mind that everyone's situation is different," warned Evonne. "It has to be an individual decision, and it's not an easy one."

"Hey," interrupted a baroque of a woman, joining the small group at the table. "Sage just asked Kasey to dance. Damn, if they put on another show like they did last time, I'll have to find someone to go home with. After watching that, AC sex doesn't have much appeal."

Donna immediately looked at Connie, who looked to the platform just in time to see Sage take Kasey into her arms. Quickly Evonne interceded. "I don't think you have to worry about that tonight."

"How do you know? They were going at it hot and heavy last time," the woman stated innocently.

"Because this is Kasey's girlfriend, Connie," explained Donna, too late.

A sharp twinge shot through Connie's chest.

"Sorry, I didn't know," the woman replied in obvious embarrassment. She left the table, but Connie hardly noticed. Her eyes were riveted on the dancing couple. The situation had unleashed a mire of emotions — anger at Kasey for not telling her, fear of a sexual challenge, anxiety over not being able to control the situation. She searched for a release. Her first impulse was to cut in on their dance. But it would certainly send the message that there was little trust or certainty in their relationship. She couldn't. As uncomfortable as it was, she would have to wait it out.

"Will someone explain to me who Sage is?"

"A friend of Sharon's," obliged Donna. "She moved here from New York."

Of course. I could have guessed as much if I were thinking more clearly. She devoted closer attention to Sage Bristo. There *was* something very alluring about her. She had thought so herself when they'd first met. But knowing the extent to which Kasey must have acknowledged it tightened her stomach into a hard knot. "She's very attractive," she admitted aloud.

Donna's honesty didn't make it any easier. "A lot of women think so."

"Masculine. But you don't lose sight that she's a woman."

"*Androgynous* is the word you're looking for," added Evonne.

"Did she date Kasey?"

Donna was doing her best to put Connie's mind at ease. "I don't think so. They met at the last party Sharon had.

I've seen Sage with a couple of different women since then, but not Kasey."

Connie stared again at the couple on the dance floor, moving slowly, talking quietly. Keeping a conversation going seemed to relieve her anxiety. "Kasey looks . . . androgynous when she's working."

"It's hard to believe that someone who can sink a number-eight nail with three swings of the hammer can look like that at night," laughed Donna, her eyes on the dancing couple.

"I know," smiled Connie, admiring how her lover looked in the tight black dress. "That's one thing that really attracted me to her. And the way she moves, like a strong, confident woman. I'm very drawn to her femininity."

"Being drawn. Is that the same thing as being turned on?" Donna asked with a grin.

"Donna!" Evonne scolded.

With a laugh at last, and a touch of momentary relief, Connie answered, "Yes, it turns me on."

"You're so feminine yourself," noted Donna. "People assume that you'd be attracted to someone more masculine, or at least to more masculine traits."

"I'm realizing now that people have a hard time with our looks. If they took time to get to know us, though, they'd find that we both have so-called masculine traits. Most women do, to some degree. Too bad they're considered masculine." Connie looked again at the platform, at her lover in another woman's arms, and suddenly she realized there was a different song playing. Sage, with both arms around Kasey, pulled her very close. The scene jolted Connie back to the reality of the situation. The anxiety that had been on hold was back, in full force. Something Kasey said made Sage laugh and loosen her hold. Their bodies separated to a more respectable position.

"Nobody's cutting in," Connie suddenly remarked.

"You're right," agreed Evonne. "It's been at least two songs."

"They'd like to see Kasey with Sage, wouldn't they?" Hesitating only briefly, Connie made her decision. "I'll be right back."

"Do you like the makeup?" Sage asked, the conversation still light.

"It's nice," answered Kasey.

"Randy did it for us. I thought you'd like it."

"I do, but ..."

The compliment was just the incentive Sage needed to take the conversation where she wanted. "Tell me something," she began. "I know you felt the same thing I did that night. You expressed yourself quite well."

Embarrassment made Kasey break eye contact.

"Why did you stop at that point?"

"I apologize. It was thoughtless and unfair."

"I don't want your apology. I want your honesty."

"Sage, there were so many factors at play that night. I hadn't been with anyone for a long time, and I was fighting my feelings for Connie. Those two factors alone made me vulnerable enough that I shouldn't have even been there. Add about five drinks that I wasn't used to and a very persuasive, attractive woman, and you have a highly sexual situation. What I felt was purely sexual. I tried to tell you that then."

"I know you did. I owe you an apology, too. I took advantage of the situation."

"I would really like to get past this. Maybe get to where we can develop a friendship. I do like you very much, but I'm in love with Connie."

"Speaking of," Sage nodded toward the edge of the platform.

After handing Tom the tape she had retrieved from the car, Connie started across the platform.

"Dedicated to Kasey from Connie," he announced, as Sage stepped away.

Sage made only brief eye contact. "Have fun," she said coolly. Her intent wasn't clear; neither was it important. Connie had a message she was about to deliver to everyone.

"May I have this dance?" she asked, to the beginning notes of "You Have It All Over Him."

Kasey slid her arms around her. "For the rest of my life?"

Connie brushed her open mouth over Kasey's lips. "For the rest of your life." Arms around her shoulders, she boldly grasped the back of Kasey's head and brought them together. Their kiss was sensuous enough for even Sharon to have felt something. And as much as they may have liked the idea of Sage and Kasey together, the women offered a loud approval of the public display.

"Something tells me the birthday dances are over," Sage said to Sharon. "You know that song is for your benefit, don't you?"

"She's got tits, I'll give her that much." Sharon nodded toward the platform. "Doesn't that bother you?"

Sage watched their intimacy. "A little. I don't regret kissing those lips, although I probably should. That's one talented, very hot woman. She'll be hot when she's *sixty*-six."

"I wish she wouldn't keep wasting it on women who don't appreciate her," complained Sharon.

"Should be classified right along with the seven sins."

They watched as Connie stared deeply into Kasey's eyes. "It does look like appreciation, though."

"Yeah, 'til her curiosity's satisfied." Sharon's tone lacked its earlier sarcasm. "I only hope it doesn't take three years this time."

Connie pressed the side of her face against Kasey's cheek. "I was wondering how much public affection you'd be comfortable with," Kasey said with a soft smile. "I think you've answered that question."

"You don't know how much I wanted to do that the first time we danced," Connie returned softly, nose to nose now. "I knew the moment you tightened your arms around me that I loved you, that I wanted you."

Kasey gazed at the pretty lips and smiled. "If you only knew how hard it was for me to let go of you that night. You had me in a slow meltdown. I knew we had to get out of there."

"What would have happened if we'd stayed?"

Kasey smiled, her lips touching lightly against Connie's ear. "The next dance would have been very physical." Slowly, sensuously she began to move her hips against Connie's, fueling the flame that the kiss had ignited.

"You're a very sexy woman," whispered Connie. "And it's a damn good thing this song is over." They kissed once again as the last notes faded. "Oh, yes. Hold that thought. I think Tom wants you to cut your cake."

With a large piece of cake in each hand, Connie approached Sage and Sharon. Their conversation ended abruptly as she neared. "Kasey's still cutting cake. I thought I'd bring these over for you."

"Thanks, Connie," Sage said with a pleasant smile.

Sharon took the plate and Connie's right hand as well, noticing the long painted nails. "Damn, Sage, will you look at these? I'll bet these nails could ruin a moment. Can't you hear Kasey now, 'Ah honey, is there something else you want to do, 'cause *this* moment is gone'?"

Only the corners of Sage's mouth curled slightly. "You no doubt thought those were screams of ecstasy."

Connie pulled back her hand quickly, as the two women laughed. "I haven't had any complaints so far," she said crisply, refusing to offer her chord hand in defense.

"Aha, there goes another misconception I've had about straight women. All along I thought they didn't do windows *or* oral sex," Sharon lashed back.

Without a reply, Connie turned abruptly and headed for the stairway.

"Cruel, Sharon," Sage said slyly. "Funny, but cruel."

Kasey met Connie's somber look at the bottom of the stairs. "Is everything okay?"

"I just need some fresh air."

Catching up with her, Kasey took her hand and led her out the back. "It's Sharon isn't it?"

Connie only took a deep breath and looked up at the stars.

"I made her promise to behave," Kasey explained, wrapping her arms around Connie's waist.

Connie leaned back against her. "I know. I guess she just couldn't resist."

"Are you going to tell me what happened?"

"No. I don't want you to say anything to her."

Kasey turned for the door. "Well, I am going to say something, and then we're leaving."

Connie took her arm. "No, Kasey. I don't want her to

think I can't take it. Don't you see? She wins then. She proves I can't take the pressure."

"Connie, I'm not going to let her treat you like that."

"Listen to me," she said, taking both Kasey's hands to keep her from leaving. "I don't want you to be mad at her. It will only make matters worse. You still have to work together."

"I am mad at her," she frowned, stepping back into Connie's arms. "But I love you more."

Connie's voice was reassuringly quiet. "And someday you're going to trust how much I love you."

The word *trust* had struck a nerve. "Now that we're alone, there's something I need to tell you, something I should have said earlier."

Having Kasey come to her without being asked was already relieving much of her anxiety. "You can tell me anything, honey."

"I hope so," Kasey took both her hands. "It's about Sage. Remember I told you I went to Sharon's party that Friday before we got together?" Connie nodded. "And that I had too much to drink. But that wasn't everything." She took a deep breath. "Sage made it clear from the beginning that she was interested. She fussed over me all night, complimented me. Everyone knew what she was doing, including me. I was trying very hard not to think about you. We danced a couple of times. The last time I was a little dizzy, so I put my arms around her neck and leaned into her." She was looking down at their hands, not yet ready to face the hurt, or whatever else she might find in Connie's eyes. "Everything just sort of happened from there."

The impending silence convinced Connie she was expected to ask the inevitable. "Did you sleep with her?"

Another deep breath from Kasey. "No, but I may as well have. We were in the hallway outside her room, basically making love standing up. When she wanted to go into her room, I stopped."

Connie stroked the backs of her long fingers over Kasey's cheek. "What made you stop?"

"You." Kasey finally looked into her eyes. "I knew what I was feeling was only sexual. It made me admit to myself that I was in love with you. I couldn't get you out of my mind, out of my heart."

"And you still made me chase you to the middle of the lake," smiled Connie, holding Kasey's face in her hand.

"I guess I needed to know how serious it was for you."

Connie pulled Kasey's arms around her. "Let me remind you."

"Kasey, there you are," Sharon said, catching them at the bottom of the stairs. "Everybody's been asking for you to sing."

"Sharon, it's too late. I'm too tired."

"C'mon, Kase, just a couple of songs. We don't get to hear you very often."

Kasey frowned and shook her head, but Connie smiled and kissed her on the cheek. "Two songs."

"Okay, c'mon," Sharon smiled.

She held Connie's hand until she had to let go. "Don't go anywhere."

"Not in your lifetime."

On her own again, Connie looked for Tom or Evonne and Donna. But before she found them, someone grabbed her arm. She turned to find herself face to face with Sharon. "Come here, I want to talk to you," she said sternly, pulling her around the corner into the laundry room.

Fighting the feeling of a child about to be scolded,

175

Connie immediately bolstered her defenses. Toe to toe, the two women stared coldly at each other. Connie again refused to break eye contact. "You don't scare me Sharon."

"Yeah? Well you're gonna pee your lacy pants when you realize that *I'm* not the biggest monster you're gonna face." Sharon pointed a threatening finger in her face. "Meanwhile, I'm going to tell you something, and I'm only going to say it once. I love that woman, and when you hurt her you're gonna pay hell dealing with me. You understand?"

She could almost feel the anger quivering through Sharon's body. Yet Connie's voice remained firm, her posture solid. "Now *you* listen. I know you love her. That's the only reason I tolerate your attitude. You've made it very clear that you don't like me, and I've been very patient with you. But let me tell you something. I love Kasey more than I've ever loved anyone in my life, not that I should have to justify that to you. And I'm not about to let anything compromise her happiness, not even you." She pressed her face so close to Sharon's she could feel the heat of her breath. "So maybe you'd better reassess the situation. I'm not going anywhere, and if her friendship is as important as you say it is, then you'd better figure out how to get along with me. Think about *that*." Pointing her own finger defiantly close to Sharon's chest, Connie abruptly left the room.

Shaky from the adrenaline and in no mood to socialize, Connie looked for a spot alone. As inconspicuously as possible she slid into a space by the end of the platform. While she watched Kasey and Jan go over their number, the confrontation replayed itself. In a strange way the whole thing was a relief. She had expected something to happen sooner or later. And now that it had, maybe things would improve. She truly hoped so, for everyone's sake.

Still deep into her own thoughts, Connie turned to find that Sage had slipped in unnoticed beside her. *Oh, perfect!* What had she done lately to warrant being tested like this? *Please, just don't talk to me.* She was relieved to see Kasey take the microphone.

Luck was running true to form for the evening, and as Kasey picked up the beat with her body, Sage said, "Have you ever seen her in action?"

"I've seen her perform, if that's what you're asking."

"For a group of lesbians?"

"No."

Sage waited for eye contact. "She really turns 'em on."

"So I've heard."

Intriguing brown eyes searched her blue for something. She searched back. But they wondered in silence until their attention was diverted.

"This is for you, Sharon. Thanks for a wonderful party," Kasey announced. Easily she swung into rhythm, her commanding voice building its excitement. Body movements and expressions added the performer's personal touch to give Sharon a most unique thank you. Connie watched the strong seductiveness as Kasey interpreted the words to Sharon's favorite song. She watched her clench her fist against her chest as the words to "No One Else on Earth" asked their questions. The confidence and strength that exuded from a clearly feminine sexuality was fascinating. The contradiction of strength and femininity was inherently sensual. No wonder she turned 'em on, as Sage put it. The combination was so ideal, yet so uncommon. Too many women, Connie decided, were afraid of exploring themselves, of developing their wholeness. It was easy to see why they enjoyed watching someone as complete as Kasey Hollander.

For a moment Connie pulled her eyes away long enough

to scan the group of women close to the platform. The faces shining with adoration teased her into a proud smile. This was *her* lover they were admiring, *her* Kasey they'd love to get next to. The feeling of pride continued happily along until her gaze returned to Sage Bristo. There her gaze was plainly challenged. The dark brown eyes were boldly enveloping every inch of Kasey's body, enjoying the movement of her hips and the glistening of perspiration on her chest as it rose and fell. There was no hint of shame to her enjoyment, even with Connie watching. Even with Kasey's choice being clear, the knowledge of how close this woman had gotten to her was terribly intimidating. *What is Sage wondering? What got her so close? Does she think she can do it again?*

"You'll have to excuse us for a minute here. Jan and I have never done this one together," Kasey explained. They huddled over the keyboard, Kasey humming, Jan testing chords. Then Kasey returned to the microphone. "She's excellent; she's got it." She turned and smiled at Jan, then looked directly at Connie and said quietly, "This is for you."

Connie's pulse quickened immediately. A flood of heat traveled the length of her body. In that one moment nothing else mattered, only the look bathed in blueness sending its shock of electricity through her. Right then there was no Sharon, no Sage. There was no one except Kasey and Connie.

"I bless the day I found you . . ." The words carried on the pure strong voice went soul deep.

Connie's heart was no longer her own. She was unaware of the other women watching as the words to the second verse entered her. She looked only at Kasey, thought of nothing but Kasey.

Then unexpectedly, Kasey held her hand out to Connie,

just as she had that night at the club. An invitation she would never refuse. She stepped up onto the platform and took her hand as Kasey began the last verse. Connie no longer existed without Kasey. "Tell me you'll love me only, and that you'll always let it be me." She pulled Connie closer and held the microphone between them. Connie knew exactly what she wanted. Jan repeated the last two phrases and together, light soft tones complementing rich and full, they finished their song. The room erupted in applause.

Kasey's smile melted into a tender kiss before she once again raised the microphone. When the room quieted she explained almost shyly, "I definitely have to go home. Thank you all for coming and making this a very special birthday. Good night."

As quietly as possible they said their good-byes and headed toward the stairs. Their exit was polite and cordial, and finally, gratefully, they entered the solace of Connie's car. It had been a long day, one filled with emotion and virtually no privacy. Connie quickly started for home. "That was beautiful Kasey," she said, reaching for her hand.

Kasey pushed up the armrest and moved beside her. "That song seemed to say everything I've been feeling. I'm glad Jan could play it."

"You sang those words right into me." Right into her soul, where the empty place used to be. The place filled now with Kasey's love. Tears formed in her eyes. "It will always be you, Kasey."

"You're more than I've ever dreamed of." Gently Kasey kissed the tear from the corner of her eye and whispered against her cheek. Her hand slowly caressed the thin silk covering Connie's breasts. "All evening I wanted to show you how much I love you."

Soft warm touches from Kasey's lips began covering the delicate skin of Connie's cleavage. "Kasey, you're making it impossible to drive." Yet, with one hand cupping Kasey's head, she encouraged the gentle nuzzling between her

179

breasts. The warmth from Kasey's hand moved slowly up under the soft dress. "Kasey, if this is a test to see how long I can take this, I'm failing it." The kisses to her breasts and neck were now relentlessly wanting. Fingers stroked the silky warmth between her legs. "Oh God, honey . . ." Connie's whisper was breathless. "Either you have to stop, or I do."

Kasey's breath was hot against her flushed skin. "I'm going to make love to you right here."

Quickly Connie pulled the car to the side of the still relatively rural road. As Kasey unfastened the seat belt, Connie laid the seat back. "I never thought I'd want anyone this much," she said pressing her mouth to Kasey's.

There was an urgency now to their desire; no crescendo of time was needed. Hours of emotional foreplay had already created a hunger demanding satisfaction. Connie moved with intent beneath her. Their kisses, void of tenderness, desperately worked toward their goal. Insistent moans met gasps of desire as their bodies struggled for contact. Suddenly Connie grabbed Kasey's hand, commanding it aggressively under her waistband where persistent fingers caressed molten desire. Breathlessly she commanded, "Now, baby, now."

Kasey's voice was lusty and low. "I love you." Easily she slipped into the depth of sweet desire. "Oh, God, I love you." Finding the place she knew perfectly, she circled it, massaged it, until gasps of excitement burst from her lover.

"Yes, Kasey . . . oh, yes baby!" Connie's words were pure pleasure. "So good, you're sooo good. Oh, yes . . . keep doing it," she breathed heavily against Kasey's ear.

Her expressions of desire brought exquisite joy. Kasey moaned with the thrill of impending orgasm. Connie shuddered against her and called out in ecstasy, "Ohhh yes, yes, yes." Tension broke its final bounds. Connie's hips rose up to take Kasey in. Deeper. Tighter. Opening fully, completely. Her cries filled the car. "I love you, I love you, I love you." Kasey covered her face and neck with tender touches from her lips as Connie's body moved against her, keeping her inside, capturing every last bit of pleasure.

She whispered the words lovingly, "Ohh, beautiful woman, you're everything to me." Kasey pressed her lips against the warm face and tasted the saltiness of tears. She strained in the darkness for an expression. Her voice was filled with concern. "What, Connie? What is it?"

Loving arms closed, holding Kasey tightly to her. "Don't ever stop loving me."

"I won't, honey," she promised, kissing away the tears. "I won't."

Kasey adjusted her position against the armrest, and Connie moved to give her more room. "I'm sorry," she said, wiping the moisture from her face. "That must have been very uncomfortable."

Kasey shook her head and smiled. "You just gave me the most wonderful birthday present anyone's ever given me."

With a hint of rare embarrassment Connie smiled and fingered the gold chain around Kasey's neck. "If I'd only known that two weeks ago." They laughed softly together, faces pressing close in the darkness. Then Connie's mood turned pensive. "How did I get so lucky, to have such an unselfish lover?"

"You get us home and I'll show you how selfish I can be."

TWENTY-SEVEN

"You made it," exclaimed Donna, as Kasey and Connie appeared around the side of the house. Each received a warm hug from Donna, then Evonne, while Sharon kept a polite distance.

Donna stepped back to check Connie's apparel. "You look good in jeans and boots."

"We had to borrow the boots. That's why we're a little late," Kasey explained.

"That's okay; they're a must. We don't want you getting stepped on. Horses sometimes aren't the daintiest of animals," laughed Evonne. "Sage is out back saddling our two ladies. We were just picking Sharon's brain about a fence we want to put up. It looks as though we're going to need your expertise, Kase. We ran into a problem."

"Hey." Sage's voice came from the direction of the corral. "Who's riding with me?"

"Sharon, aren't you riding?" Kasey asked.

"No, I've got bad cramps today. I don't feel like it."

Kasey looked at Connie. "Would you want to ride with her? I could help them with the fence problem, then you and I could ride later."

The idea was less than thrilling, of course, but held its own sort of irony. She was obviously not the person with whom Sage had hoped to ride, and if she could get past her worry of looking stupid in front of her it might prove to be an interesting ride. "Sure," she decided. *Why not?*

"Connie's gonna ride," Donna called back. "We'll be right there."

"You'll be fine," Kasey said reassuringly. "You probably ride better than I do."

Connie worried that the apprehension Kasey sensed was apparent to everyone. "I don't know. It's been quite a while."

Evonne started in the direction of the corral. "Don't worry. Sage likes to ride Blaze, and wherever Blaze goes, Sassy follows. They're inseparable."

"A lot like their owners," Donna inserted with a smile.

"You won't have to worry about controlling her. Just ride and enjoy yourself," Evonne finished.

"Okay. I'll be all right."

Entering the corral, Connie looked admiringly at the two magnificent chestnut horses. "They were raised together. The original owner tried to sell them separately at first," Donna was explaining, "but they wouldn't eat. He had no choice but to find someone to take them both. We were perfect."

"They're beautiful animals," remarked Connie.

Sage handed the reins to her. "Here you go."

"Connie, this is Sassy." Evonne lovingly stroked the velvet nose to tender their introduction.

Connie ran her hands down the powerful neck. "Hi, Sassy. I hope you're a gentle girl 'cause I'm a bit rusty." Sassy lowered her huge head and gently nudged Connie's chest.

"I think she likes you already," Donna laughed.

Sage was already in the saddle, so after a few more get-acquainted strokes, Connie decided it was time. With the reins and horn in hand she planted her left foot in the stirrup and began her mount. In the fraction of a second, with a breathtaking thud, she found herself on her back in the dirt, looking up at the saddle hanging awkwardly on the side of Sassy's barrel chest. Sharon burst out laughing. Connie looked up in time to see the remains of a smile on Sage's face before Kasey helped her to her feet.

"Are you all right?" Kasey asked, while Evonne dusted off her white shirt.

"What happened?" It wasn't clear if what she was feeling was embarrassment or indignation.

"The cinch was too loose." Evonne's reprimand was polite. "Sage you forgot how tricky Sassy is."

Donna righted the saddle and explained as she tightened the cinch. "Sassy always takes a deep breath and holds it when you try to tighten the cinch. You have to slap her on the belly and tighten as she exhales."

Sage's tone held an undefinable edge. "I forgot," she said, sitting tall and aloof atop Blaze.

Connie's tone remained forgiving. "That's okay. I should have double-checked it."

"You ready to try this again?" Donna asked with a smile.

"One more time." Connie brushed the seat of her pants and mounted, this time with no difficulty. She gave Sassy a number of thank-you strokes for holding so still.

"You ready?" Sage asked.

"I'm no Dale Evans, but let's go."

Just as Evonne had said, with no prompting from Connie, Sassy followed Blaze out through the gate. As she passed, Kasey reached up and patted Connie's thigh and gave her an encouraging smile. "If I'm not back by dark send the posse," joked Connie. Even Sharon smiled.

At a slow trot the horses carried the women over the hill behind the barn and down the path leading through a clump of trees. Connie, feeling more comfortable in the saddle, marveled at Sage's expertise. "For a big-city woman, you sure are at home on a horse. You handle her very well."

They wound their way along the path, Sage not responding immediately. "There's more to New York than New York City," she returned, passing through an opening in the trees. They paused at the edge of a large field, adjacent to the trees. "I had access to a large horse farm upstate."

A nice easy trot and comfortable conversation. Maybe this won't be so bad after all. "I used to ride a lot, but it's been at least ten years since I was on a horse."

"Maybe it would help if you thought of it like having sex with a man — the more you relax the less painful it will be."

Connie locked her blue eyes into the steely brown stare. It was apparent now that the situation wasn't intended to be a comfortable one. Apparent, too, was the correctness of her instinct regarding the loose cinch. Sage hadn't forgotten. "Do you dislike me because of Sharon or because of Kasey?"

"Neither." Her voice was a cold wave, her stare constant. "I've been with women like you. You read like a cheap romance novel."

Abruptly Connie broke eye contact. Pulling hard on the left rein, she turned Sassy back toward the trees. An argument was imminent unless she left. Sassy cooperated until they reached the edge of the path. There she began to sidestep, fighting the rein. Blaze called to her as Sage turned her toward the field, and that was all it took. Despite Connie's best efforts at control, Sassy ignored her rein and turned to follow Blaze. A futile effort to hold her back ended when Sage suddenly broke Blaze into a full gallop. Sassy bolted, almost throwing her rider. With only one foot still in the stirrup and one hand desperately gripping the saddle, Connie struggled hard to regain her balance and keep from being thrown. Painfully she strained to pull herself forward. She squeezed hard with her knees. Finally, centered again in the saddle, she managed to regain her foothold in the stirrup.

The instincts of so many years ago took over. She pushed against the stirrups, rising up out of the saddle long enough to settle into the rhythm of Sassy's gallop. Now she was riding, riding like she knew how, her legs strong and sure, her posture true. Giving Sassy full rein and encouraging the speed of her long, smooth stride, she caught up to Sage.

Running alongside now, Sassy matched Blaze stride for stride as they galloped across the field. A surprised Sage looked over and kicked Blaze into full speed. Sassy responded automatically. Connie was actually beginning to enjoy the challenge now. Across the rest of the field they raced, making a wide turn at the far side, and then racing all the way back. Although she didn't expect her to admit it, Connie suspected Sage was also starting to enjoy herself. Slowing to a trot, Sage led them through another clump of trees to another clearing made up of several hills and valleys.

They stopped at the top of the first hill to let the horses rest. With her anger subsided, Connie's curiosity got the best of her. She chanced a question that risked further insult. "When you said you've been with women like me, what kind of women were you referring to?"

Sage looked at her as if she was either amazed at the question or at Connie. With a characteristic delay, she looked down at Blaze and straightened a braided section of mane. Connie wondered if Sage was deciding how to, or if she should, answer her question. Connie waited patiently while Sage gazed out over the view from the hill.

Finally Sage began. "Women who appear to be so straight in every part of their lives, then secretly slide into bed with someone like me. They have to have the husband to keep the appearance of a normal life. They want financial security and no risk of losing the kids." She hesitated, stroking Blaze again. "But they crave the emotional intimacy and good sex that only a woman can give them. So" — she finally looked at Connie with a cool, unemotional grin — "if you're into beautiful women and flings, there are plenty of them out there. You just have to be careful not to do something stupid like fall in love with one of them."

She ignored the reference. "Like you did?"

"No." Her response was unusually quick, her eyes glazed with ice. "I let her keep me ... like a mistress." Sage waited, frozen in an unexpected stare-down, for a reaction she never got. "You gonna ride or talk?"

Connie suddenly broke the stare and nudged Sassy down the hill.

They rode for a long time with no further discussion, climbing the hills, racing the valleys. *Strange woman,* Connie thought, glancing over at Sage. There was a coolness, a confidence about her that bordered on arrogance. Yet unexplainably, it wasn't intimidating. It only made Connie look closer. And what she saw was something in her smile, when Sage did smile, that was a definite contradiction. She watched her as they rode back and wondered if she would ever really know her. More peculiar was her desire to, despite the way she was being treated.

* * * * *

The sounds of the barn took up the silence. Brushes raked over the slick backs of the horses. The two women worked silently until Donna came hustling in. "Wow, you're back in one piece and we didn't even have to send out the posse."

"Were we gone too long?" Sage asked.

"Long enough for us to decide to eat without you. I'll finish up here," offered Donna. "You two go get cleaned up."

Sage continued to brush Blaze. "No, I'll stay and help you."

"Go ahead, Connie. I think Kasey's getting a little worried."

"Thanks, Donna." Walking by Sage on her way out, she said quietly, "For the record? You're wrong about me." The words probably meant nothing to Sage, but she felt better for having said them.

During the rest of the day as the women interacted, Sharon and Sage kept an accommodating distance. Donna and Evonne, however, proved thoroughly delightful. They were warm and honest. They maintained a closeness full of smiles and friendly touches that made Connie feel liked right from the beginning. She found them to be kind, understanding women, and she felt welcome in their home and in their lives. It was that feeling of acceptance that made her understand how important these two women were to Kasey, and how important they now were to her.

She entered the family room where everyone had gathered, bringing drinks for Kasey and herself. "Ooh," she groaned, bending to sit on the floor in front of Kasey. "With all the running we've been doing, I didn't think I'd be this sore. But I'm already starting to feel it."

"It's a whole set of muscles you didn't know you had."
Evonne smiled.

"No gymnastics tonight, my friend," Donna winked at
Kasey. "But after you've been together a while, you'll get
used to those laid-back nights when nothin's happenin'."

Kasey only smiled and began massaging the muscles in
Connie's neck and shoulders.

"It sounds like you think we do it all the time,"
returned Connie with a smile.

Kasey jumped in before Donna could respond. "No, it
sounds like that's what they used to do when they were
first together." When everyone laughed, the atmosphere took
on a lighter, easier air. Teasing, it seemed, was acceptable,
and that was fine with Connie.

"Yeah, tell them about the time Evonne's boss almost
caught you," suggested Sharon.

"We laugh at it now," Evonne began, "but it wasn't so
funny at the time. I was working late at the office, and
Donna met me there with something to eat. My boss had
left hours before. Well, one thing led to another . . ." A red
flush spread over her soft round face. Her maternal eyes
twinkled with unexpected mischief. Everyone already had a
picture in their minds and started laughing quietly in
anticipation. Donna put her hand over her face as Evonne
continued, "And we were on the floor, in the act, when I
heard the outside door open. You never saw two women
dress so fast in your life. I pushed Donna into the closet
just as my boss opened the office door." Even Sage was
laughing aloud. "I still wonder what kind of expression I
must have had on my face. He said something about me
working so late and that he had forgotten something, and
then he left. I don't know what I would have done if what
he had forgotten had been in that closet." The women were
lost in laughter, but Evonne wasn't finished. "Wait, there's
more. When I opened the closet door, Donna burst into

189

laughter so hard she couldn't talk. Finally, she managed to drag me over to the mirror behind the door. I couldn't believe my eyes. My hair was standing straight up, and my bra wasn't fastened so I was a lot lower than usual. Only one button on my blouse was buttoned, and it was in the wrong hole, and I was holding the closure to my pants together!" Connie was laughing so hard she was wiping tears from her eyes, and Evonne still wasn't through. "But you know what was really funny? He never once mentioned it. I can't imagine what he was thinking. He must have thought I was drunk."

The laughter eventually died to giggles, but only after it had loosened the tensions that had bound the earlier moments of the day so tightly around the women. It gave them all a common ground, something they shared and enjoyed together. More open now, unhindered by self-induced barriers, they began to share stories. They told of near misses and times when they'd been caught. Although none of the stories matched the comical extreme of Evonne's, they were fun and even enlightening.

Sage told about getting caught parking with a woman while she was in college. "We were going at it pretty heavily, all the windows were steamed opaque, when there was a tapping on the driver's window. When I rolled it down, I was staring into an officer's flashlight. 'We were just talking' was more a joke than an explanation. He warned us that he'd better never see us on that street again." The women waited for the other shoe, and Sage obliged. "He did catch us again — doing the very same thing — the very next night."

The story proved to be as revealing as it was funny. It exposed a strong thread of defiance running boldly through Sage's personality. Connie was quick to recognize it, storing it away for the future as a piece of the puzzle. Sage's life, she suspected, embodied experiences far more extreme than that — episodes too revealing to share. For despite the rumors she inspired, everything about her seemed grossly understated.

Kasey's hands began their massage once again. Connie leaned forward, resting her arms on her knees, making it easier for Kasey to reach her back. "Mmm, that feels so good."

"Kasey gives the best back rubs I've ever had," remarked Donna.

"She's got great hands," Evonne said.

Donna teased the top of Connie's head on her way to the kitchen. "Like she doesn't know that."

Evonne's face flushed. "I didn't mean it that way."

"We know, we know," Sharon laughed. "But she is good enough to charge for her services."

"Don't tempt me," warned Kasey. "I've done enough of them to be a rich woman."

"Sounds like I'm the only one here who hasn't had one," Sage said, sounding suspiciously innocent.

"Yeah, well I think you got her deluxe treatment." Sharon smirked, leaving no misgivings of innocence.

Connie felt the hands suddenly stop against her back and turned her head in time to see a glare, sharp as a dagger, hurled at Sharon.

The message pierced its mark. "I was only joking."

Kasey rose and walked over to Sage, but her chastisement remained directed at Sharon. "I don't think anyone thought it was funny." She reached down, tossed a small pillow on the floor, and grasped Sage's arm. No smile warmed the firm tone. "Your turn."

"I was just kidding too, Kasey."

"I'm not. Lie down."

Sage stood defiantly, face-to-face. Everyone watched silently. "You sound like one tough woman."

"Tough enough to *put* you on the floor if I wanted to embarrass you."

"Don't mess with her, Sage," Sharon warned.

191

Quietly and seriously Sage explained, "Look, I don't want to cause a problem."

"You won't." Kasey couldn't keep the faintest smile from her lips. "Just lie down."

The challenge past, Sage relented and settled on her stomach on the floor. Kasey knelt over her buttocks and placed strong hands on her shoulders. It was the first time Connie'd seen Kasey react so strongly. But knowing her stubbornness, it didn't surprise her. She continued watching as Kasey reached down, pulled the shirt from Sage's jeans, and with one hand swiftly unfastened her bra. A move she knew only too well.

A surprised Sage raised her head and looked back at Kasey. "Maybe we should do this in private."

"Otherwise," Kasey replied, pushing Sage's head back down on the pillow, "you'll end up with a bruise."

"I'm gonna throw the Frisbee for Cooper before it gets dark," Sharon said.

"Okay, but make sure you stay on the west side of the house," warned Donna. "Our neighbor threatened to shoot any of the animals that get on his property."

"Too bad you can't have that bastard arrested," Sharon grumbled as she passed.

"Just be careful," Donna emphasized.

"I will. Come on, Coop."

"That's why we're putting up a wood fence instead of the wire," Evonne clarified. "A little privacy won't hurt either."

"We'll rent the power auger Thursday," Kasey said. "And I'll get the extra bit in case we run into major roots in that one spot."

"Okay, then just show us how to set the posts, and Evonne and I can do the rest," replied Donna.

"You sure you don't want help?"

"No, you're doing enough by digging the holes."

192

"You still with us, Sage?" Evonne gave a quick wink to Kasey.

Sage only moaned softly, looking thoroughly content under Kasey's skillful hands.

Connie watched the beautiful hands she knew so well pressing into Sage's faded blue shirt. She had never seen their movements before, only felt their effects. Strong and commanding, the tanned arms and hands with their prominent veins worked their magic. Such a strange feeling, she thought. *Could it possibly be sensual without being sexual?* She didn't know how else to describe it. But now it was finally clear what Kasey was doing, why she had insisted so strongly. She needed to do this, in front of her friends, in front of her lover, to prove that physical contact could happen between them and not be sexual. A proof, Connie suspected, Sage wasn't ready for. However, she'd bet Sage wouldn't exchange places with anyone right now. The hands continued their work, covering the length and breadth of Sage's shoulders and back several times.

"I don't know how you can do that so long, Kase. I try to give Evonne massages, and I get tired so fast," Donna admitted.

"I tell her she should do it more often," laughed Evonne.

"That's right," added Kasey. "It'll build your endurance." Her sly smile got the laugh she was looking for as she pressed against Sage's back and rose from her position. "Okay, your complimentary session is over. The next one will cost you dearly."

Her eyes still closed, Sage's response was little better than a murmur. "Next time I'll give you anything you want." Kasey reached down and playfully slapped the back of her head.

Returning to her seat, she draped her arms over Connie's shoulders and wrapped her in a tight embrace. She nuzzled into her neck and whispered, "I love you, cowgirl."

"I know," she said, snuggling in with a sweet smile.

"Okay, girls," announced Sharon, emerging from the kitchen, "I tired Coop out, so I guess it's time to go home. Damn, Kasey, what did you do to Sage?" The realization that the body on the floor hadn't moved an inch, made everyone laugh. "Sissy," teased Sharon in a soft motherly tone. "Time to get up, sweetie." Even Connie had to smile.

"Mmm, turn out the light," Sage mumbled sleepily.

Still in a playful mood, Sharon leaned down and began tickling Sage's sides. She jumped into consciousness immediately, squirming her way out of Sharon's reach. Again the laughter was at her expense as she leaned up against Donna's legs with a sheepish smile. "Dammit, Sharon."

"C'mon, you can go back to sleep when you get home. Just don't think you're gettin' any massages from these hands."

Sage quickly fastened her bra and rose to her feet as Sharon hugged Evonne and Donna. They waved their good-byes to Kasey and Connie on their way out the door and headed for the car.

"Could she really have put me on the floor?" Sage asked.

Sharon smiled. "In a heartbeat."

TWENTY-EIGHT

The spaghetti noodles were just right. Connie pulled the pan from the stove. "Kase, dinner's about ready," she announced, giving the sauce a quick stir and taste.

Kasey called from the living room, "Let's eat in here." She switched the TV to their favorite news station and removed the laundry basket from the couch. With a pile of folded towels stacked to her chin she started for the linen closet. They had chosen not to go to the cabin this weekend and to catch up on domestic chores instead. She wanted to be available in case Donna called for help on the fence.

All of a sudden, a familiar name on the TV captured

Kasey's attention. Walking back into the room, she was shocked by the recognition of the faces on the screen. "Both women were shot and killed this morning in their yard, allegedly by a neighbor," the voice reported.

"Nooo!" Kasey screamed. She stared at the screen — straight into the faces of Donna and Evonne.

At the sound of the scream, Connie raced into the room. Kasey was sitting like a frightened, wounded animal on the coffee table. "What, Kasey? What is it?" Her focus followed Kasey's eyes to the screen, where she tried to understand what was happening.

The newscaster continued. "The women had lived together in a lesbian relationship for the past eleven years, which may have been a contributing factor in their murders. Evonne Koch, the older of the two women, is the mother of two adult children. At this time police are questioning an elderly man living next to the women. We will have more on this story as the facts become known."

"Oh, God, no!" Connie exclaimed. "This can't be happening."

"No, no," Kasey repeated as she stood. "It's not them." She paced erratically around the room, running her hands nervously through her hair. "It's not them," she said, shaking her head.

Connie reached for her arm, but Kasey pulled away. "No, no," she said, moving away from Connie's efforts, as if avoiding consolation would invalidate the news. "I've got to go," she said, anxiously scanning the surface of the coffee table with her hands.

Connie swiftly grabbed the keys from the end table. "Where Kasey, where? Where do you have to go?"

Kasey covered her eyes with her hand and shook her head. Suddenly she bolted through the kitchen and out the back door. Connie began to follow, but stopped, catching the screen door on its way back. She watched Kasey's aimless steps eventually take her to the back fence. Then, through her own tear-filled eyes, she watched Kasey painfully pound the boards with her hands, yelling no over and over again.

Tears streamed down Connie's face. In helplessness she witnessed her lover's anguish, until the ringing of the phone pierced their private shock. Its ring, minuscule by comparison, made answering it seem vastly unimportant. She ignored it. But the voice called persuasively from the machine. "Kasey, Connie, this is Sage. *Please* pick up. I really need your help." She stayed on the line, waiting.

Dutifully Connie picked up the receiver and heard herself say, "This is Connie."

"Were you listening to the news?"

"Yes."

"Believe me, you're the last person I want to bother, but Sue isn't home. Sharon's hysterical. I don't know what to do with her. I've got her car keys, but I don't know where the key to the gun cabinet is. She's threatening to kill him."

"It's such a shock. Kasey's . . ." She hesitated. "She's taking it very hard." Connie paused again, wanting to make the right decision. "We'll be there as soon as we can."

She approached Kasey, now with her hands gripping the top of the six-foot fence, her head down. She was sobbing. Sliding her hands up over the top of Kasey's, Connie pulled them from the boards and wrapped them and her arms around her. For the next few minutes she held her. All she could do was offer what strength she had and the comfort of her arms. There was nothing she could say that would help. Finally, she whispered, "We've got to go to Sharon. She needs you."

They traveled the distance to Sharon's in silence. Connie held Kasey's hand as she drove. Kasey stared out the window and periodically wiped her eyes.

"I don't think it would help for Sharon to see me," Connie said, pulling in the drive. "You go ahead. I'll wait here. If you think you ought to stay, come let me know and I'll go back home." Kasey nodded and squeezed her hand, then hurried to the front door. Connie watched until she disappeared inside, then leaned her head back and tried to make some sort of sense of what had happened.

"Kasey." Sage's voice was soft as she embraced her. "I'm so glad you're here. Are you okay?"

"I can't believe it."

"I haven't had time to think about it yet." They released their embrace as Sharon stormed up the stairs. "Here." Sage handed Kasey a set of keys. "This is what she's looking for."

Kasey slipped the keys in her pocket as Sharon burst into the room. There was urgency in each step, indignation in her eyes, and a rifle in her hand.

"Kasey, good. C'mon, we gotta hurry. C'mon." She grabbed Kasey's arm forcefully, but Kasey stepped in front of her. "No, Kasey! Get out of my way!" she shouted. "I gotta get that bastard. He hurt 'em Kase, he hurt 'em bad."

Sharon continued pushing toward the door, but Kasey stayed in front of her. "It's okay, Sharon, it's okay. The police have him now." Tears ran down her face. She struggled with her own composure, trying to muster the strength for two.

But Sharon, shocked and angry, wasn't easily calmed. "It's not okay. It's not! They need me." She began to shake, tears spilling from her eyes as she repeated the words, "They need me." But, she knew their futility now.

"He can't hurt them anymore."

Sharon looked into the sorrowful eyes and cried out

loudly, "Oh, no! Oh, God, Kasey!" Suddenly their deaths were reality. "Why? Why?"

Kasey put her arms around Sharon's shoulders and embraced her. "I don't know. I sure as hell don't know." In the comfort of Kasey's embrace, Sharon loosened her grip on the gun. Kasey slipped it away and held it out to Sage. Sharon buried her face in Kasey's shoulder and began to weep. Kasey gripped her hard, rocking her gently. "Shhh." The words were almost impossible to form now. "No one can ever hurt them again." With her last bit of control, she whispered, "They're together. They'll always be together."

Isolated in her own emotions, Connie didn't see Sage approach the car until she tapped on the window. Her intrusion was unwelcome, but with rain falling consistently now, she motioned her in. "I won't tolerate any indignities, Sage, so don't even try."

"Dammit, Connie. Two very fine people are dead and my best friend is hysterical. What kind of a person do you think I am?" She hesitated, a look of annoyance quickly disappearing. "I wanted to thank you for getting here so quickly."

"I'm sorry." Her apology offered, Connie turned her head to the window, leaned against the headrest, and closed her eyes. The ensuing silence was uncomfortable, the mixture of emotions almost unbearable. Anger, frustration, and anxiety were all taking their toll. But the one emotion tearing at them the hardest now was sorrow. It was probably the only one that could bring the two of them together.

Sage spoke softly. "I'm sorry, too, for a lot of things. I just don't know what to say right now."

Connie continued to stare blankly out the window. "The

only thing we can do is try to help the two people we care most about get through this somehow." She turned to find Sage, still staring out the window and nodding in agreement. Sage finally turned to meet Connie's eyes.

"Do you think they'll be all right in there alone?" Connie asked.

The concern Sage saw touched her. "They've been through so many crises together. They were there for each other when Sharon's brother was killed and when Kasey's mom died. And they helped each other through both breakups. I trust they'll know how to get each other through this. We just have to let them need each other right now."

Sage leaned her head back against the window, tears making their way slowly down her face. "How could this happen? How could that bastard hurt such good people?"

"I don't know. I never thought I'd see such hatred against someone I knew." Tears filled her eyes as thoughts of their warm hugs and gentle smiles came to mind. "They were so nice to me, from the first moment I met them. I'll never be able to tell them how much that meant to me." Tears flowed steadily now. "I almost lost my mother this summer. You'd think I would remember to thank people right away, to tell them how much I appreciate them."

"No one expected anything to happen to them."

"That's just it. Things can happen so unexpectedly. And then it's too late to say what's in your heart or make things right with someone."

Long, slender fingers dragged their tips up and down the window track. Sage watched them as if they were someone else's. Only a few feet apart, the women grieved privately, silently. Connie's words had hit home; their personal implications awakened Sage's well-protected conscience. The animosity she had been holding for this woman was suddenly exposed for just what it was — a selfish, impudent cover for her wounded pride. It was a difficult thing to put into words. She was embarrassed for having lacked the benevolence to handle the situation with Connie more maturely. Once again the silence between them had become uncomfortable.

The rain stopped. Connie rolled down the window and breathed deeply of the cool damp air. Although it momentarily lifted her depression, she felt guilty for enjoying it. She had lost sight of her grief for only a second. Now it was back and overwhelming. Mixed with shock and disbelief, there was no relief for it and no one to share it with, unless she and Sage could get themselves on level ground. "Sage, I know this is uncomfortable; it is for me, too. Maybe it would help if we talked about something else. Maybe we should talk about the problem between you and me." Sage stared back at her with no distinguishable expression. "I know what happened between you and Kasey."

"She told me she was single."

"She was. I'm not faulting you for that at all. I probably would have done the same thing. But I also know Kasey would like to be friends with you, and realistically that just isn't going to happen. Not unless you and I can get along, and trust each other."

Before Sage could respond, the front door opened. Both women watched as Kasey approached the car. "I'm sorry," she said, peering in the driver's window. "I didn't mean for you to have to wait so long."

"Is Sharon okay?"

Kasey nodded, swollen eyes very serious.

Connie touched her cheek tenderly. "How about you?"

"I'll be all right. It'll help us both if we can stay busy. I called Evonne's daughter."

"Good."

"The family's gathering over there. Sharon and I'll go over. Maybe there's some way we can help. Are you two going to be okay?"

"I'm going to ask Sage over to the house." She looked to Sage for an affirmative nod. "We've got a lot to talk about. You do what you think is best about Sharon."

"Okay." The faint smile Kasey gave Sage was the best she could offer.

Connie leaned toward the window, kissed Kasey on the lips, and whispered, "I love you." As they watched the retreat of Kasey's saddened form, she realized how it may have looked. "I didn't do that to be rude to you."

"I know. You did it because she needed it."

Neither was very talkative on the way to Connie's. Sage and Connie each did a lot of soul searching in those few miles. Not until they sat at either end of the couch, a cup of coffee in their hands, did Sage begin to open up. "You're being much too nice to me for as nasty as I've been to you."

"Isn't there a saying about keeping your friends close and your enemies even closer?"

"You consider me an enemy?"

"I don't want to." Connie peered at her over her cup as she took a sip. "Maybe there's something we can say here that will help us take the first step toward understanding each other."

"I think we have taken the first step." Her face softened, the sharp outline of her masseter muscles finally blending into her cheeks. "Since I first met you I've tried very hard not to like you. I wondered if you had even the slightest idea how lucky you were to be with Kasey." Her unabashed eye contact changed abruptly. Sage lowered her eyes. "But what you said in the car really hit me. I would never want it to be left like that." Once again her eyes lifted. "The truth is, I do like you. I think Kasey has excellent taste in women."

"That's funny," smiled Connie. "I thought the same thing at the party when I first realized who you were."

Honesty and the change in subject had a lifting effect on both women. Sage smiled for the first time all day. With her arm draped comfortably along the back of the couch, she looked noticeably more at ease. "Are we really into true confessions here?"

"Why not? We've come this far."

Sage nodded. "It would have been very easy for me to fall in love with Kasey."

"It was easy for me." Her eyes searched Sage's reflectively. "I had no idea what was happening until it was too late."

"Too late?"

"By the time I realized I was in love with her, I couldn't stand a day going by without seeing her. When I told Kasey, it scared her and I thought I'd lost her. That's when you met her."

"Things are making a whole lot more sense now." As she hesitated, Connie began to see for the first time a part of Sage's personality emerge that she had suspected was there all along. Without even moving, Sage seemed to have drawn closer. "I don't want this to sound egotistical," she was saying, "but I've never had a woman go that far before and stop. I didn't know what to think. Actually, I thought about nothing but her until I found out about you."

"Then you could concentrate on disliking me." She acknowledged Sage's nod. "Is there anything I can say here that would help?"

The corners of her lips turned ever so slightly. Her eyelids narrowed gently. "Maybe you could tell me that she's very selfish or has a bad temper or displays obnoxiously annoying little habits." She had Connie smiling now. "Or better yet, tell me she's terrible in bed."

Connie raised her eyebrows with a gentle laugh. "Can't do it."

"I didn't think so."

"She is very stubborn, though."

"I saw that last weekend."

"She also takes on too much responsibility at one time, and she hates to cook."

"There it is," Sage smiled. "I'll have to find someone else so I don't starve."

At last, having shed much of their personal burden, they laughed. However temporary it was, it tempered the sadness of the day. Laughter, it seemed, had a way of healing, of soothing the sorrowed soul. So indeed they had taken a first step, and maybe more, toward a more healthy relationship. One they were both in need of.

Sage looked intently into Connie's eyes. "Thank you."

"For what?"

"For letting me see how lucky Kasey is."

"You're really very sweet, aren't you? I guess I should be glad that I met her before you did." Before she could offer Sage another cup of coffee, the phone rang. Connie answered it in the hall.

Minutes later Sage watched her pass in front of the couch without a word. "Kasey?"

Connie nodded. "They're dealing with the media. As if grief isn't enough to deal with."

"Maybe it'll help take their minds off the pain."

"Like we've been doing. I suppose so, temporarily." Connie stared out the window. "Kasey told me that when she lost her mother the funeral arrangements and all the responsibilities only delayed it. Later, she finally had to face the loss on her own."

"We all face loss in our own way, sooner or later."

Focused in their stares, they struggled to do just that until Connie finally spoke. "I still can't believe it happened." She paused. Sage was leaning forward on her thighs, still staring at the floor. "Should I turn on the news?"

Sage lifted her head. "It might help answer some questions."

Connie rejoined Sage on the couch and waited quietly through the last few minutes of a program and impending commercials. Then the news anchor began the story they dreaded. "Our top story tonight is the double murder this morning of two local women at their home in a quiet rural neighborhood." The report continued with a picture of Donna and Evonne smiling happily with their arms around each other. He reported the information from the earlier broadcast concerning their ages and lifestyles and where they worked. Then the picture changed to film clips taken during the day. "Police were called to the scene about ten this morning by a neighbor who said she heard gunshots and saw another neighbor leaving the scene carrying a rifle."

The reporter pointed out the familiar surroundings, the yard, the house, the postholes that Kasey and Donna had dug only days before. Horrible visions of gentle women taking their last painful breaths began washing over the weak dam Connie'd placed on her emotions. The only relief to the nagging ache was a fresh flow of tears.

"It is unclear," the reporter was saying, "whether the murders were the result of a boundary dispute. The women were in the process of installing a fence separating their property from that of the suspected killer."

"It wasn't over the boundary. Those holes were a good foot inside the boundary stakes." Anger, rumbling in the pit of Sage's soul all afternoon, found its way to the surface. "It was about playing God — about eliminating what you can't change. There is no justification for that kind of hatred."

The camera focused on Evonne's daughter, Jenny. Through obviously guarded emotion, she fielded the reporter's questions. Yes, there had been threats. Yes, they were reported to the police, even as recently as yesterday.

She was asked if the animosity had anything to do with the women's lesbian lifestyle. "Donna and my mother were gentle, loving people. There would be no reason on earth for anyone to ever harm them," she answered as the guard on her emotions began to fail. Blinking back developing tears, pursing about-to-quiver lips, she turned and walked away.

The coverage switched again. With the use of a cane, the suspect could be seen laboriously making his way into the police station. "One questions what could possibly have prompted this elderly man, in his obviously disabled condition, to allegedly pick up a rifle, travel the distance needed, and murder his neighbors," stated the reporter.

"That son-of-a-bitch isn't any more disabled than I am. Look at him. You saw him. He wasn't having any problem walking last weekend."

Connie got up and switched off the set. "It won't matter, Sage. It doesn't change the facts."

Her words sounded dangerously resolute. "Somebody *should* shoot him."

"And then they'd be playing God, wouldn't they?" Words that, no matter how true, were incapable of dulling the sharpness of this kind of pain — this kind of anger. She reached out to Sage and carefully stroked the soft wavy hair.

As the tension loosened, Sage leaned her head against Connie's slender hip and bore her anger in silence.

TWENTY-NINE

Two days passed filled with anguish and sorrow and many strained confrontations with the media. The funeral would be somewhat of a blessing today. It needed to be over, at least to the extent that a funeral was capable of bringing an ending. They needed to say good-bye.

The wills had been quite explicit, with all arrangements decided ahead of time. Amazingly, there was no opposition from either family. Donna and Evonne would be buried together. Reverend Mary Griffin, who had blessed their union, would now bless their departure. The families had decided on only one ceremony, to be held at the graveside.

Everyone who met at the funeral home to form the procession quietly and privately saw them for the last time and said their good-bye. So many tears in so little time. There hardly seemed to be anything left to cry with. Yet still the tears came, and Connie suspected they would for quite some time.

Close friends and family were seated in the first two rows. Inadvertently, Connie found herself sitting between Kasey and Sharon. But it was neither the time, nor place, to worry about something so trivial. The service had begun.

Donna's brother spoke first. He shared memories of them growing up together; some happy, some sad. "I remember how confused and emotionally torn I was when my parents forced Donna to leave home. They had found out she was a lesbian. She was seventeen, I was fourteen. I remember not knowing why she had to leave. Somehow I thought it was something she could control. I called her where she was staying and cried and pleaded with her to come home. Donna was crying too and kept trying to explain what was happening. We had been so close. In a strange way it made me feel unimportant to her. I felt like she had abandoned me. It wasn't until we were adults that I realized what an impact prejudice and ignorance had had on our lives. We became close friends once again. And now, prejudice and ignorance has taken her from me again." Tears now streamed steadily down his face. "And I don't know when I'll get to see her again." He tilted his head back and took a deep breath, an attempt to regain control enough to finish. With a quivering lip he managed. "We cannot let their deaths be in vain. This may have been a battle lost, but we all must realize that the war goes on."

Connie and everyone around her were blotting their eyes at this point. But Sharon was having an exceptionally difficult time. Her head was buried in her hand, and her body shook as she tried futilely to control her crying. The hand closest to Connie was resting on her leg, clenching a

Kleenex. Without reservation, Connie reached over and took her hand. Face still covered, body racked with emotion, Sharon opened her hand to Connie's. The gesture hadn't gone unnoticed. A few seconds later Kasey found Connie's eyes. She squeezed her hand and acknowledged her compassion as one more reason she loved her.

Evonne's daughter, Jenny, now stood before them. She cleared her throat and began. "There are no words that could tell you how much my mother has meant to me. I have only begun to feel what losing her and Donna is going to mean in my life. I learned so much from them. I learned how important love is, and I learned honesty. I learned how to be strong and how to give. They taught me so many things, things that are so valuable to me that I am making sure to instill those values in my own children. It saddens me that Mom and Donna will never see how much that meant to me. And it saddens me that my children will grow up without their love and example. But along with all the wonderful things I gained from them, I also learned about hatred and bigotry. I watched them quietly fight it every day. They were well aware of the war, as Jeff called it, but they never felt like they were called to be on the front line. They tried to live a quiet, peaceful, normal life. They were loving and giving and happy. They were friendly, probably to a fault." The tears were apparent against her cheeks now, her voice unsteady. "But for some unexplainable reason, they've been taken from us. I guess if I've learned anything at all from their deaths, I've realized that, whether we know it or not, we are all in this war." She was openly crying now, speaking in short phrases. "We've got to put aside . . . our complacency . . . find ways to eliminate this hatred . . . If we don't . . . everyone will suffer."

As Jenny sat down into her husband's embrace, Tom inconspicuously started the tape in the portable stereo. It was one he and Kasey had made a couple of years ago. Everyone knew the impossibility of Kasey singing today. The tape was perfect. Her beautiful voice soon filled the tent, reaching into the hearts gathered there, offering words almost too painful. "If I'd only known it was the last walk in the rain . . ." Connie recognized the beginning of the song Reba McIntyre had dedicated to her band members killed in an accident. She knew the words would say what so many in that tent were feeling, but couldn't say.

The soothing sound and poignant words filled the thick fog of silence enveloping the gathering. Pastor Griffin stood between the coffins, head lowered, silently praying. A long minute passed before she spoke. " 'If I had only known . . .' But we don't know most times. We can't. We're not God. We don't know His plan, or His schedule. So we have to love while we can, use every precious moment possible to express our love. If there is a problem, we must resolve it. If there is a misunderstanding, we must correct it. We must not let time lull us into believing that later will be better. If you should thank someone, do it now. If you need to forgive someone, or tell someone you love them, do it today. Don't wait, don't put it off." She paused for a moment, possibly to let the full impact of her message be felt. "That was their legacy to us. The life Donna and Evonne lived together. A life of quiet example, of courage and love. Losing them has made us all look at their example closely and personally."

Connie realized, during that moment, how much it was helping to concentrate on her face, on her message. She studied this woman of God, with her soft loving eyes and powerful words.

"I'm going to ask everyone right now to take the hand of the person on either side of you. This is the hand of a special being whom God has made. They may be black or white, male or female, gay or straight, Protestant or Catholic. They may have money, they may have none. But there is one thing to be sure of, they have a soul. A soul created in love, to be nourished by love. Squeeze that hand now in acknowledgment of that precious soul. You don't need to know anything else about that person unless you wish. But know this. Each of us needs to love and to be loved, to be happy in this world."

Again she paused, closing her eyes prayerfully. Raising a hand above each coffin, she tilted her face upward and said, "Pray with me now as we say good-bye to our friends. Dear God, we know Your love is immeasurable and unfailing. Help us now to entrust these precious souls, Donna and Evonne, to Your eternal loving care. Through Your Holy Spirit, give us the strength and courage to continue loving and forgiving despite our terrible loss. We will never forget them or stop missing them, but we'll look forward to seeing them again with You. In our Lord Jesus' name, we ask You now to take them in Your loving arms and grant them eternal happiness. Amen."

As people let go of hands and wiped their eyes, she ended the service with these words: "Stop now for just a second. Take a deep breath. Come back to the reality of what life is all about. Cherish every moment, every breath, every soul. Be everything you can be. Don't wait. God has given us His love as an example. Go now and love one another."

THIRTY

Kasey snapped down the last leg, and Sharon set the last of the rented tables in place in her basement.

"I picked up the chairs yesterday, Kase. They're still in the Blazer." She tossed the keys across the table. "Pull it around back and we'll unload them next. Then we can take a break."

Kasey wanted to believe Sharon was wrong about the handling of the case and that today's meeting wasn't necessary. But it had been three months since the murders, and there was still no mention of a hearing or trial date in the media. Through daily contact with Jenny, Sharon was aware of the families' concerns, the most recent of which was the prosecutor's apparent lack of conviction in speaking out about the case. Jenny's concern was now theirs. Was it a professionally-masked homophobia that made him less than enthusiastic with his assignment?

Two folding chairs in each hand, Kasey misjudged the clearance and banged her right hand against the edge of the sliding door. "Shit! Dammit Sharon! I thought you said you'd fixed this damn thing." She slammed the chairs down and rubbed her bruised knuckles. "It still doesn't slide all the way open."

When she didn't hear Sharon's typical sarcasm in response, she looked over and found her on the phone. The look on her face made Kasey smile despite the pain. It was one of those looks your brother might give you when you said something in front of your parents that you'd never get away with otherwise. Sharon — stifled. It was comical.

Kasey returned with four more chairs, being careful this time to clear the narrow opening. So many times she had wished this whole thing could be over. She needed normalcy in her life, if there was such a thing. She didn't mind helping the families. That wasn't it. Everyone had been wonderful about volunteering their time and efforts. Connie helped get their financial affairs in order. Sage and Sharon had been taking care of the animals. She, herself, had dedicated every weekend to helping organize and sort household belongings, a difficult and emotional task. Decisions as to what to keep, what to give away, what to sell, were emotionally draining. She had never even finished going through her mother's things. Sentiment and logic were often in conflict. It would be a long process. But what they all needed soon was some sort of closure.

"I knew it." Sharon hung up the phone and stood abruptly. Hands on her hips, she exclaimed, "My instincts were right."

"What happened?"

"Crawford's lawyer was granted a delay to allow his client to check into a hospital. He claims Crawford's health is failing. Additional stress from a hearing will put his life in danger. The prosecutor didn't even challenge it, and there's no date set for a hearing."

"How could they have kept this quiet so long?"

"*Why* is even more important."

"I wonder if they have any idea of how closely they're being watched by the gay community?"

"They will after today."

Despite the sensationalism of a case involving lesbians, it had run its natural course in the media. Linda Sterns, director of the state Gay and Lesbian Task Force, agreed that it was important to keep the media's attention. But she advised against hit-and-miss tactics. She volunteered her services for today's meeting to help plot an objective, organized approach.

Sharon introduced a plain, bespectacled Linda Sterns to forty-five women determined to do whatever was necessary to ensure justice.

"As many of you know, Sharon and I have been active in the local and statewide organization for years now. We are constantly trying to encourage more lesbians to get involved with our organization, either openly or behind the scenes. It has not been an easy task. For years gay men have been the mainstay of our organization. And until recently, we have had very few women willing to be openly involved. What we have also found, unfortunately, is that until something like the recent tragedy occurs most don't see it as a personal fight. It has to hit home first. And now it has, or you wouldn't be here today." She looked into serious, intent faces of women touched by tragedy, many of whom had never before attended a meeting like this. "What

I'm here to tell you is that you must see the problem in its entirety. You must recognize its enormity and what impact your efforts can have on its resolution." The faces were open, waiting for guidance. "My belief is that that recognition, that understanding, will be easier to see at first right here in your own city, your own neighborhood, your own workplace. *Then*, the confidence in the power of your voice and your numbers can be felt on a larger scale. Many women, including lesbians, are now beginning to realize their social and political power on a national level. But for you, for now, it's got to start here. Here is where it is most important."

Like a college professor welcoming a new batch of first-year students, Linda Sterns scanned the attentive faces. "Now that you've been properly inspired, we should get to the task at hand." A smile finally lightened her face. "Sharon has arranged you into small groups to discuss ideas for actions you think appropriate. We have outlined the problem to be acted upon on the large paper hanging on the wall. When we meet again as a whole, a spokesperson from each group will list your group's ideas. Then we'll categorize them and begin the tedious task of prioritizing and decision making. Sharon?"

Sharon listed the groups and where they were to meet. "Remember, this is a brainstorming session. That means every idea that is spoken must be listed. No decision about validity is made during this part. I'll come and get you in thirty minutes."

When they met again as a whole they went about the task of formalizing the final list. The ideas ranged from the absurd to the obvious. A public execution by masked vigilante lesbians was out. But finding a public venue for openly discussing the issue was an obvious choice to be placed high on the list. They decided that a march in front of city hall, showing interest from all over the state, would get the media involved again. Plus, it would probably result in at least one on-camera interview. Getting a couple of people on local television and radio talk shows was another choice high on the list. They would push for getting both a representative from the families and one from the gay community on to discuss the full ramifications of the crime. Sending letters to the editors of the two area newspapers was also placed on the final list, as was a long-term plan of increased openness in the community. But probably the most dramatic decision was to investigate, and to aggressively pursue, a change in prosecutors.

Connie left the meeting with a lot of good feelings about finally being a part of some positive action. It was against her basic nature to sit back and not even try to change things. She hated the feeling of powerlessness. Yet she hadn't forgotten that the extent of her involvement was not solely up to her anymore. Kasey had made no indication she wanted to be involved any further. With Donna and Evonne's deaths an ever-constant reminder of the extent of society's intolerance, fear was a natural, understandable response. But the same fear that seemed to paralyze Kasey served to infuriate Connie Bradford. She fought succumbing to it, fought letting hate and ignorance have their way without a fight. She knew she must find some way, some positive channel into which she could direct her anger, *with* Kasey, preferably. But if not, she would do it silently and discreetly alone.

"I realized something today, honey," Connie began. "I've realized that Sharon, despite her own intolerance and opinionated principles, is a wise woman."

Kasey lifted her eyebrows in surprise.

"She knows an important truth, and with all she holds sacred she wants you to see it too."

"What are you saying?"

"She knows that lesbians who look like you and me and gay men like Tom and Michael have the power to ultimately tip the scales." Her eyes bore seriously into Kasey's. "There are a lot of us, aren't there?"

"More than anyone could imagine."

"Tucked safely into the nooks and crannies of society."

Kasey nodded.

"What would happen if something in the chemical makeup of homosexuals reacted with some mineral in water, and without a choice, we all turned green?"

Kasey laughed at the classic speculation. "Heterosexuals would turn very pale and shit their pants. But lucky for them, we do have a choice."

"But don't you see? Coming out like that is the only weapon that can prevent what happened to Evonne and Donna from happening again."

"Not enough would ever come out to have that kind of impact. And for those who did, it would just get more dangerous."

There was a long silence as they got ready for bed. Finally, Connie pressed the subject further. "Are we going to be a part of the demonstration next week?"

"We'd be essentially coming out."

"I know."

Kasey saw that she had made it again, the invitation no other lover had ever made. She had offered the possibility Kasey refused to contemplate. "No, it's not up to me. You'd better think this out more thoroughly. The media will be there. Someone from work is bound to see you." Kasey popped her head around the corner of the bathroom. "Are you really ready to come out to Jack?"

"I've thought about it."

"What if his reaction is bad and he makes life miserable for you at work . . . or fires you?"

"I can always go out on my own. I've played with the idea before. The loss of benefits would be the hardest adjustment." Smiling to herself, she added, "I already have one account."

Kasey emerged from the bathroom wrapped in a towel. "Yes, but it doesn't pay very well."

"Oh, yes it does." She pulled the spread neatly to the end of the bed. "That account has made me the richest person in the world."

She felt Kasey's arms encircle her waist from behind. Her lips were warm and tender on her neck. They hadn't made love since the funeral, and over the weeks the conflict between Connie's understanding and her patience had become noticeable. When they talked about it, Kasey had difficulty putting her feelings into words. It wasn't easy for her to talk about the haunting thought that if only she had gone to help that weekend maybe she could have done something to prevent the murders. Even harder was dealing with the guilt she felt from even a fleeting thought of gratefulness that she wasn't there. It was easy to see, placed in that perspective, that sexual gratification seemed selfish and unimportant to her.

Intimacy though, had been important, and they'd spent many nights just holding each other and talking. And there'd been other nights when Connie had awakened to find Kasey on the other side of the bed crying quietly. She would spend the rest of the night comforting her, holding her, trying to give her enough peace to sleep. It was a deep pain, not easily soothed. She understood why someone like Kasey might never be able to come out.

Connie pressed her cheek against Kasey's and leaned back into her embrace. "I want you to know I'm very proud of you. I fell in love with you partly because of the depth of your emotions and your passion. And I know, with that comes a high vulnerability to pain. Courage is a very personal thing. It doesn't have to be a debate on *Oprah* or telling the truth to the Pentagon or even to your boss. It can be as quiet as walking away from a gay joke or as singular as telling a parent or a best friend. Or as powerful as loving a woman. You are a courageous woman, Kasey."

The soft voice whispered against her ear, "I love you."

Connie turned to her lover and embraced her. "We need to start taking care of us, honey. I need to feel close to you. I need to make love with you." As she spoke, the soft warmth of Kasey's lips along her neck began sending their message through the rest of her body. "Oh, yes, I need you. I need to feel you against me." The towel fell quickly, along with Connie's T-shirt. The touch of Kasey's warm skin brought instant arousal. Connie's whisper brushed against Kasey's ear. "The first time I felt your skin against me I thought I was in heaven. I didn't think anything could feel that good" — she nestled into Kasey's embrace — "until I came to you."

"I thought you were too good to be true." Kasey pressed her face into the beautiful softness of Connie's breasts, caressing them with the smoothness of her cheeks.

At last, with a moan wrenched from her soul, Kasey released her grief from its hold on her. She finally let go, giving up the guilt and destructive emotions that had controlled her for months. Donna and Evonne would not want to have this effect on her life. There was nothing more she could do for them. She resolved to remember them with love and to think about their humor and their smiles whenever the sadness came.

What she did now had to be for her and the woman in her arms. Her love for Connie had grown day by day. It was time to show her the depths of that love, with hands knowing and tender, with the heat of her mouth, warm against the soft skin, with her lips, against every inch of delicate flesh. She would show her.

Connie's slender fingers slipped through the golden hair, grasped Kasey's head, and pulled her mouth tightly to the softness of her breast. Lips touched the yielding nakedness with increasing excitement. A sigh, long and soft, blended into the most rapturous moan as Kasey stroked and loved the tenderest skin of Connie's breasts with her tongue. Nipples, taut with desire, were pressed into her mouth. The pleasure it brought was evident in ardent breaths. "Yes, my love, I've missed you so."

The raspy breathing stirred sensations deep in Kasey and warmed her body throughout. She lifted her face from the softness into eyes charged with desire. They closed with the tilt of her head, as she offered her mouth over the graceful curve of Connie's throat. Arms tightened around strong shoulders, pressing their need around her. Her body quivered at Connie's yielding. Trembling limbs, warm with excitement, moved exquisitely against her own. Kasey's hands lingered over the undulating hips, moving with them, on them, wanting more than she could reach. Connie brought their mouths together with kisses slow and deep, in direct contrast to the growing urgency of their bodies.

Restraint beyond her now, Kasey pulled them down onto the bed, sliding them together like exact pieces of a puzzle. She wanted this woman with every part of her being, loved her from the deepest part of her soul. Murmurs of desire quickly became gasps of desperate need. Hearts pounded hard against each other, the movements of their hips becoming fierce in demand of satisfaction. The hunger of their mouths, opening deep, tested the edge of their desire, stronger now than when it was new, completely void of reservation. Frantically they reached for each other, bathing themselves in warm, silky wetness. Pleasure expressed itself breathlessly, sounded with unique voices of love and joy, told with quickening gasps how close to ecstasy they were.

Each touched the other with perfect knowledge of what the other needed. They felt with explicit sensitivity the paralyzing pleasure they were giving. Their bodies opened completely, filling each other with an incandescence as intense as fire at combustion, fanning the coals until they burst into flames. They tendered the flames into a tremendous explosion. Their bodies rocked with equal rapture, lifting sublimely in ecstasy until the spasms of pleasure softened into warm, breathless acquiescence.

For a long time they remained, mind and body deep inside each other, unwilling to compromise their bond. Finally Connie spoke softly, whispering from her soul. "You're part of me. You fill me in the place right next to my soul."

"That's where I'll always be."

THIRTY-ONE

The signs read STRONG ENOUGH TO KILL — STRONG ENOUGH TO STAND TRIAL and OPINIONS ARE LEGAL — MURDER IS NOT and JUSTICE WEARS A BLINDFOLD. They were carried by a crowd of over two hundred and fifty gays, including only a sprinkling of men. The sight of that many lesbians gathered openly in front of city hall was exhilarating. Sharon was rightfully proud of her efforts.

The media were there as expected, and they would be for the duration. After all, there was always the possibility of an exciting confrontation to juice things up a bit. And whether they wanted it or not, the interview they got from Evonne's daughter offered an in-depth emotional look at the personal impact of a hate crime. When she was through, Donna Nichols and Evonne Koch had become more than two lesbians. They were the mother, grandmother, sister, and friend that anyone could relate to. Their deaths were no longer just the statistics of a hate crime, but heinous, senseless murders, the effects of which were devastating, and extended far beyond the gay community.

When the reporter asked Sharon why they felt it necessary to demonstrate, her reply had been diplomatic but direct. "To be a woman has always meant a struggle for equality, a struggle for visibility under the law. To be a minority woman has meant an even greater struggle. As lesbians we are minority women, a minority that has always been fearful of the struggle. But after the death of our sisters, we realize that we too must be willing to fight for our rights. If *we* don't believe in our worth, how can we expect others to?"

The reporter, unmoved in his professionalism, asked, "Don't you trust that the law is going to be exercised properly in this case?"

"Laws are only words in a book. Unless they are enforced, they are worthless. Throughout history there have been incidences of discretionary enforcement. We're trying to make sure that this won't be another."

A lot of homework had gone before her answers, hours of discussion on all possible questions. She had hammered out the most effective replies and memorized them. She had done her job well, as had the others. It left them all with a strong feeling of accomplishment and empowerment. This would make a difference. Maybe not a big difference, and surely not in itself, but it was a start. A good start.

"Damn, Sharon. You ought to go into politics." Sage smiled as she rejoined the women on their designated path.

"Maybe that's my niche in life." Sage was in the middle of another compliment when Sharon grabbed her arm. "I don't believe it!" She was staring out into the parking lot.

Sage focused her attention in the same direction. "I do."

Emerging from between the parked cars, looking feminine and beautiful and holding hands, were Kasey and Connie. The perfect flowers to complete a very special arrangement. And more important, a very personal decision made. Sharon could contain her excitement no longer. She ran to the edge of the parking lot, where to everyone's surprise she grabbed Connie, picking her up and twirling her around twice. "You're wonderful. *Wonderful!*" she exclaimed. "How did you do it?"

"It wasn't me. She's ready."

Adding to Connie's amazement, Sharon kissed her on the cheek. "Yes, it was you," she said, as she allowed Connie's feet to find ground once again.

Then with unmistakable emotion, she grabbed Kasey in a tight embrace. She didn't say a word. But Kasey sensed every bit of her emotion, and it brought tears to her eyes. "Hey," Kasey said, clearing her throat. "Did we miss your interview?"

"Yeah," Sharon returned, wiping her eyes quickly with the back of her hand. "But we can watch it on the news tonight." There was a happiness in her eyes and her face that Kasey hadn't seen for quite some time. "We'll tape the whole coverage at my house tonight, okay?"

The cameras continued to roll. The couple continued their greetings undaunted. The decision had been made. Society would have their glimpse, however small, of one more facet of lesbianism. And they would be the better for it.

THIRTY-TWO

Leaning back in her office chair, Connie stared out the sixth-floor window and reflected on how her life was changing. The world would now have to relate to Kasey and Connie, a lesbian couple. Different, she thought, even from relating to her as an individual gay woman. Each affected the other in decisions, in actions, and reactions. More complicated than she had realized. *Challenging* was a better word. But as her mother had taught her, anything worth having is worth working for. And work on it she would. She wanted their life together to be as wonderful and fulfilling as it could possibly be. Anything it took to make it so would fall prey to Connie's logical, systematic efforts that had begun the day before the demonstration when she decided to ask her boss to lunch.

They settled at their table, and Jack, to the point as usual, began. "You've never asked me to lunch alone before, Connie. I suspect you have something you'd like to talk to me about. Am I right?"

"Ordinarily, for both personal and professional reasons, I would not put you in the position of having lunch with me alone. You're right, I need to talk with you. I didn't know a better time or place to do it."

"Stop worrying about how it looks and just tell me what's on your mind. I should warn you though, as much as I appreciate your work, I can't even consider a raise until after the first of the year." His attention was divided between Connie and the menu.

"No, it has nothing to do with money. It's of a more personal nature." The waitress interrupted to take their orders. She continued, "I'm going to be involved in a demonstration tomorrow that will undoubtedly be covered by the media. I wanted to make you aware of it so that you wouldn't be surprised if you saw me on the eleven o'clock news." She watched the familiar brown eyes darting back and forth between coffee preparation and her.

"Look, Bob has always been very active in the Democratic party, and I'm a staunch Republican. Don's an active, born-again Christian, and I'm a Catholic. I mean what I've said, Connie. Politics and religion are your personal business. As long as it doesn't affect your work for me, it's none of my business." She admired his straight-ahead, direct approach to everything. You always knew where you stood with Jack. It made what she had to do much easier.

"I know you mean what you said. I've never seen you deviate from it. That sense of fairness is one of the things I admire most about you. That's probably why I feel the need to explain this to you. It wouldn't be fair of me to put you in a position of being caught off guard if someone else told you before I did." She wanted to hurry and ease the puzzled look on Jack's face, but she had to wait while they were served.

As the waitress turned to leave, Jack impatiently asked, "Is this an abortion clinic demonstration that could get ugly or something?" He was no doubt envisioning bailing her out of jail in the wee hours of the morning. The possibility made her smile.

"No." Her thoughts returned to their purpose. "It has to do with demanding that the man who killed two women a few months ago be held over for trial."

"Right. I remember. I haven't heard anything more about that." There was noticeable relief in his posture. He delved into his sandwich.

"Exactly. It's possible that he may not be charged, or that lawyers will plea-bargain it down to therapy."

He spoke between bites. Connie nibbled. "How can that happen? I thought there was a witness."

"There was. His lawyer is claiming that he was provoked by their lifestyle. That his strict Christian morals were pushed to the edge. Observing their sinfulness day after day drove him insane. At least that's what I've gathered from news reports."

"Mmm, that's right. They were lesbians, weren't they?" His coffee cup stopped momentarily before it reached his lips. "How did you get so involved in this?"

"I knew the two women. Remember the personal day I took? I went to their funeral." She wondered if she needed to go further. His face registered no connection. While the courage remained, she added, "Except for family members, probably everyone at the demonstration will be gay." She felt an instantaneous relief for having followed through.

Jack put his sandwich down, wiped his mouth with the napkin, and leaned back in his chair. He chewed his last bite of food while staring into Connie's unyielding eyes. The information was computing. Finally, with eyes equally unyielding he asked, "You're a lesbian?" Connie nodded. "Since when?" His mind was probably searching for the last time he had seen her with Greg.

"Probably all of my life. I finally realized it when I fell in love with a woman."

There was a look of total bewilderment on his face as Jack struggled to understand. "Look, tell me if I'm out of line, but you're a remarkable-looking woman, with a mind and personality to match. You could have any man you wanted. Why would you want to be a lesbian?"

"It certainly isn't something I planned, nor is it a choice — that is, if I want to be happy. I fell in love with a very talented, loving, wonderful person who loves me more than I can fathom. That person just happens to be a woman. I have never, ever been this happy. I only wish other people in my life could understand and share my happiness."

His eyes remained riveted on hers. A slight nod of his head indicated his acknowledgment. "This must be one helluva woman."

Her smile said as much as her words. "She sang at the open house with Tom."

His expression, however subtle, showed more surprise than she had ever seen from Jack. "Now you have blown my mind. That's about as far away from a man . . ." There was a pause as Jack thoughtfully sipped his coffee. Connie wondered if there would be more questions. "Despite knowing how much Shirley and I like you, it must have been a tough decision to tell me something so personal."

"It was," she admitted. "I even questioned why I felt it necessary. But unfortunately, what gay people do in their bedrooms can affect their jobs."

"But if this were about a man, it wouldn't matter. You never would have felt compelled to tell me about it." He watched Connie nod. "You certainly never felt you had to tell me about your personal life with Greg."

"Not any more than you would offer personal information to a business associate."

"I'm sorry it's like that, Connie. Maybe things will change. There is a lot more acceptance for alternate lifestyles now than there was even five years ago." She sensed an almost parental concern. She studied the lines of his face. He was concerned. He was trying to reassure himself that maybe her life wouldn't have to be difficult and complicated just because she fell in love with a woman. Beneath his efficiency and unemotional approach to life was a caring sincerity.

"Things would certainly change a lot faster if there were more people like you. I really appreciate your open-mindedness and your fairness. Not everyone is lucky enough to work for someone like you."

"Thank you, but I can't take all the credit for that. My mother worked hard, alone, to raise a good boy. I've always wanted her to be proud of the man I grew into."

"I'm sure she is." Her smile lightened the mood considerably. "Does this mean I still have a job Monday morning?"

Jack smiled and glanced at his watch. "Not unless you're back to work in fifteen minutes."

THIRTY-THREE

"What do you think our chances are for first degree?" Kasey asked, claiming the seat next to Sharon in the lobby of the county building.

"I'd like to say real good, but the truth is, I don't have a clue. Haskin isn't even making any predictions, and he's read a lot of juries in his career."

"I'll sure be glad when this is over." Kasey sipped water from a paper cup. "I give you a lot of credit, lady. You did an awful lot of work organizing people and keeping them focused and informed."

"There's really no way of knowing how much effect we

actually had, but it proved to be great therapy for me. I really needed something important to keep me busy; something I could dedicate my thoughts and efforts to. I think it's kept me sane. I don't think you realize how valuable it is to have someone to go home to, someone who's always there for you, to take your mind off things."

"Yes I do. I even encouraged Sage to stay with you when she was worried about overstaying her welcome."

"You did? I am glad she stayed. She's not there as much as a lover would be, but she's been a great help."

"Anybody for gum?" Jenny offered as she joined them. "What do you think about the defense not putting the old man on the stand?"

"Smart move," answered Sharon. "Haskin would have pushed his buttons up there. The jury would have seen firsthand what an ill-mannered, egotistical bigot looks like. They had to try to protect the image they were trying to sell."

Jenny leaned her head back against the wall. "The conservative Christian, tormented daily by the image of a sinful lifestyle. I thought I would throw up. How could a jury possibly swallow that when they heard three different witnesses testify to three separate unprovoked threats?"

"Not being able to produce more than one favorable character witness couldn't have helped their case much either," noted Kasey.

"They're relying pretty heavily on their professional witnesses. Their psychologists had to convince the jury that consistently witnessing what he conceived as sinfulness could suddenly push him over the edge," Sharon explained.

"A concept that assumes the jurors believe he's a kind and virtuous person," added Kasey. "Did he kill out of hatred, or out of a disturbed sense of righteousness?"

Sharon nodded in agreement. "It comes down to twelve people who don't know anyone involved making a decision they can live with."

"It's hard for me to look at it with any objectivity."
Jenny's face was drawn, her eyes tired. "I couldn't believe
how much psychology was involved, even in seating the jury.
Whom do you dismiss, whom do you keep? Jurors we were
confident with were dismissed by the defense. The questions
were geared to weed out gays, families of gays, feminists,
and anyone who's lost someone to violence. And Haskin was
trying to avoid seating older men, Republicans, and anyone
raised south of Ohio. It all seems like a chancy guessing
game."

"Like I said, even Haskin wouldn't make any predictions." Sharon stood up to stretch her legs. "By the way,
has anyone seen him this morning?"

"He's been in the conference room with his assistant
most of the time," Jenny answered. "He talked with us when
we first got here. He said the jury so far has only asked for
the police record of when the threats were reported. He
thinks that's a good sign. He's guessing that if they come
back in before noon it'll mean rejection of insanity and
probably a verdict of murder in the first or second degree."

As the women continued talking, the conference room
door opened. John Haskin emerged and started down the
hall toward them. His slim, straight figure with its stately,
deliberate gait exuded confidence. He spoke softly and
precisely. "The jury is coming in."

The women stood. Jenny looked him straight in the eye
and took a deep breath. "This is it." John Haskin smiled
slightly and nodded. He took her arm and escorted her
toward the courtroom. Kasey and Sharon silently made the
journey with them. They dealt privately with their anxiety
and their hope.

Once again they settled into their usual seats in the
all-too-familiar courtroom. The actual trial had taken the
better part of two weeks. One day had been lost to a sick
juror, another to an unexpected scheduling problem for the
judge. Kasey and Sharon had alternated days whenever

possible to avoid losing too much work time. Poor Troy had had a rough two weeks, and Kasey promised to make it up to him.

The room began to fill quickly. People came in from all over the building, wherever they'd been waiting. Both Donna's and Evonne's families were present, as well as a number of friends and neighbors. They stood as the judge and jury filed into the room, then took their respective seats.

Judge Bradley addressed the jury. "I understand we have a decision in this matter. Is that so, Mr. Foreman?"

"It is, your Honor."

It was all happening so quickly now. After months of anguish and anticipation, it was about to be over in a matter of seconds.

Judge Bradley asked the question he'd asked hundreds of times. "What say you?"

All eyes were riveted on the foreman as he spoke. "In the matter of Crawford *versus* the People, we find the defendant guilty on two counts of murder in the first degree."

Jenny grabbed her sister and hugged her hard, tears spilling down her cheeks. John Haskin tipped his head back and finally smiled as the Judge asked, "So say you all?"

"Yes," was the unanimous response.

Sharon squeezed Kasey's hand. "Yes," she repeated emphatically. "Yes."

Kasey watched the old man, waiting for a reaction as the jury was polled. His face never changed. He stared stoically at each one as each juror individually confirmed the decision. *What kind of a mind can allow such a horrendous act?* she wondered. *How can something so innocent as love for another generate such hatred?* She still couldn't comprehend it. Her mind tried to override her emotions, to accept justice as a satisfactory closure. *Life in prison for a sixty-seven-year-old man. What does that mean?*

Five years, eight years? Is that suffering enough to pay for two precious lives and all they touched?

Handcuffs were placed on the old man's wrists. As they walked him past Kasey and Sharon, he looked directly into their eyes, one after the other. From an arm's distance away he snarled, "Too bad you weren't there."

There was no description for the feeling in the pit of Kasey's stomach. She took Sharon's arm. "I'll be at the phone," she said, hoping to dilute the poison of his words. "I promised Connie I'd call when it was over."

EPILOGUE

"You know, even though we have a shitload of stuff to do, I'm glad you made us do this," smiled Kasey. She reached over and took Connie's hand as the car merged onto the highway.

With their second anniversary only days away, Connie had arranged a special weekend for the two of them at the cabin. Everything else was on hold. She and Kasey were going to be completely, and wonderfully, unavailable.

"Life was becoming much too routine, you have to admit. Daily duties, things we feel we have to do, have kept us from spending some quality time alone. Really, I guess I'm feeling a little selfish."

"Whatever your reasons, I'm glad we're going."

They filled the next three hours with talking and singing and teasing, things they hadn't done enough of for a long time. Connie realized, looking at Kasey's face as they turned in to the drive, how long it had been since she had seen that beautiful carefree smile. She had first seen it right here, that first weekend; it was the smile that said *I don't have anything else to think about, except enjoying this and you*. What a beautiful smile, and it was coming right at her. Kasey wrapped her arms around her, hugging her and turning her at the same time. "I need this."

"I almost forgot how much I do too."

"C'mon, let's hurry and unload so we can watch the sunset."

The lake, bathed in scarlet and dressed in early fall, shared its freshness with the silhouetted figures on the hill. Kasey and Connie spoke in brief interludes as if not to interrupt the grand show before them. Then as darkness nudged away the day and softened the hues, Connie spoke with a radiance of her own. Her arms wrapped around Kasey, she said softly, "I want to always be with you." The silhouettes changed to profiles, their edges beginning to blend into the night. Again she spoke. "Will you marry me?"

The soft scarlet space separating their lips disappeared, fusing their forms into one softened outline. Moments later, their separating figures barely visible against a quickly darkening sky, Connie asked, "Was that a yes?"

"You're serious." Kasey's smile was barely distinguishable. "You're not pregnant, are you?"

"Not unless you're a better impersonator than Randy."

Kasey ran her fingers gently through the dark shiny hair and said nothing. She looked down for a moment, and then she removed her mother's diamond from her hand and slipped it on Connie's finger.

"Oh, Kasey," Connie whispered.

The look in Kasey's eyes was very serious now, and her smile was gone. The words were softly spoken. "Yes, I'll marry you."

About the Author

Marianne Martin resides in Michigan as a writer and professional photographer. Before turning her hobbies into a career as a photojournalist with *The Michigan Women's Times*, she taught for many years in the public school system. An athlete since childhood, she has been a successful basketball and softball coach at the high school and amateur levels, and field hockey coach at the collegiate level. She has spent all her not-so-leisure time in recent years working with her father to design and build her own home. The experience, wrapped around bruises, splinters, and a powerful sense of achievement, has taught her more about herself than she ever would have guessed.

SUBSTITUTE FOR LOVE by Karin Kallmaker. One look and a deep kiss... Holly is hopelessly in lust. Can there be anything more? ISBN 1-931513-62-7 $12.95

MAKING UP FOR LOST TIME by Karin Kallmaker. 240 pp. When three love-starved lesbians decide to make up for lost time, the recipe is romance. ISBN 1-931513-61-9 $12.95

NEVER SAY NEVER by Linda Hill. 224 pp. A classic love story... where rules aren't the only things broken. ISBN 1-931513-67-8 $12.95

PAINTED MOON by Karin Kallmaker. 214 pp. A snowbound weekend in a cabin brings Jackie and Leah together... or does it tear them apart? ISBN 1-931513-53-8 $12.95

THE WAY LIFE SHOULD BE by Diana Tremain Braund. 173 pp. With which woman will Jennifer find the true meaning of love? ISBN 1-931513-66-X $12.95

GULF BREEZE by Gerri Hill. Could Carly really be the woman Pat has always been searching for? ISBN 1-931513-97-X $12.95

THE TOMSTOWN INCIDENT by Penny Hayes. 184 pp. Caught between two worlds, Eloise must make a decision that will change her life forever. ISBN 1-931513-56-2 $12.95

BACK TO BASICS: A BUTCH/FEMME EROTIC JOURNEY edited by Therese Szymanski—from Bella After Dark. 324 pp. ISBN 1-931513-35-X $12.95

SURVIVAL OF LOVE by Frankie J. Jones. 236 pp. What will Jody do when she falls in love with her best friend's daughter? ISBN 1-931513-55-4 $12.95

DEATH BY DEATH by Claire McNab. 167 pp. 5th Denise Cleever Thriller. ISBN 1-931513-34-1 $12.95

CAUGHT IN THE NET by Jessica Thomas. 188 pp. A wickedly observant story of mystery, danger, and love in Provincetown. ISBN 1-931513-54-6 $12.95

DREAMS FOUND by Lyn Denison. Australian Riley embarks on a journey to meet her birth mother . . . and gains not just a family, but the love of her life. ISBN 1-931513-58-9 $12.95

A MOMENT'S INDISCRETION by Peggy J. Herring. 154 pp. Jackie is torn between her better judgment and the overwhelming attraction she feels for Valerie. ISBN 1-931513-59-7 $12.95

IN EVERY PORT by Karin Kallmaker. 224 pp. Jessica's sexy, adventuresome travels.
ISBN 1-931513-36-8 $12.95

TOUCHWOOD by Karin Kallmaker. 240 pp. Loving May/December romance.
ISBN 1-931513-37-6 $12.95

WATERMARK by Karin Kallmaker. 248 pp. One burning question . . . how to lead her
back to love?   ISBN 1-931513-38-4 $12.95

EMBRACE IN MOTION by Karin Kallmaker. 240 pp. A whirlwind love affair.
ISBN 1-931513-39-2 $12.95

ONE DEGREE OF SEPARATION by Karin Kallmaker. 232 pp. Can an Iowa City librar-
ian find love and passion when a California girl surfs into the close-knit dyke capital of the
Midwest?   ISBN 1-931513-30-9 $12.95

CRY HAVOC A Detective Franco Mystery by Baxter Clare. 240 pp. A dead hustler with a
headless rooster in his lap sends Lt. L.A. Franco headfirst against Mother Love.
ISBN 1-931513931-7 $12.95

DISTANT THUNDER by Peggy J. Herring. 294 pp. Bankrobbing drifter Cordy awakens
strange new feelings in Leo in this romantic tale set in the Old West.
ISBN 1-931513-28-7 $12.95

COP OUT by Claire McNab. 216 pp. 4th Detective Inspector
Carol Ashton Mystery.   ISBN 1-931513-29-5 $12.95

BLOOD LINK by Claire McNab. 159 pp. 15th Detective Inspector Carol Ashton Mystery.
Is Carol unwittingly playing into a deadly plan?   ISBN 1-931513-27-9 $12.95

TALK OF THE TOWN by Saxon Bennett. 239 pp. With enough beer, barbecue and B.S.,
anything is possible!   ISBN 1-931513-18-X $12.95

MAYBE NEXT TIME by Karin Kallmaker. 256 pp. Sabrina Starling has it all: fame, money,
women—and pain. Nothing hurts like the one that got away. ISBN 1-931513-26-0 $12.95

WHEN GOOD GIRLS GO BAD: A Motor City Thriller by Therese Szymanski. 230 pp.
Brett, Randi, and Allie join forces to stop a serial killer.   ISBN 1-931513-11-2 $12.95

A DAY TOO LONG: A Helen Black Mystery by Pat Welch. 328 pp. This time Helen's
fate is in her own hands.   ISBN 1-931513-22-8 $12.95

THE RED LINE OF YARMALD by Diana Rivers. 256 pp. The Hadra's only hope lies in
a magical red line . . . climactic sequel to *Clouds of War.*   ISBN 1-931513-23-6 $12.95

OUTSIDE THE FLOCK by Jackie Calhoun. 224 pp. Jo embraces her new love and life.
ISBN 1-931513-13-9 $12.95

LEGACY OF LOVE by Marianne K. Martin. 224 pp. Read the whole Sage Bristo story.
ISBN 1-931513-15-5 $12.95

STREET RULES: A Detective Franco Mystery by Baxter Clare. 304 pp. Gritty, fast-paced
mystery with compelling Detective L.A. Franco   ISBN 1-931513-14-7 $12.95

RECOGNITION FACTOR: 4th Denise Cleever Thriller by Claire McNab. 176 pp.
Denise Cleever tracks a notorious terrorist to America.   ISBN 1-931513-24-4 $12.95

NORA AND LIZ by Nancy Garden. 296 pp. Lesbian romance by the author of *Annie on
My Mind.*   ISBN 1931513-20-1 $12.95

MIDAS TOUCH by Frankie J. Jones. 208 pp. Sandra had everything but love.
ISBN 1-931513-21-X $12.95

BEYOND ALL REASON by Peggy J. Herring. 240 pp. A romance hotter than Texas.
ISBN 1-9513-25-2 $12.95

ACCIDENTAL MURDER: 14th Detective Inspector Carol Ashton Mystery by Claire McNab. 208 pp. Carol Ashton tracks an elusive killer. ISBN 1-931513-16-3 $12.95

SEEDS OF FIRE: Tunnel of Light Trilogy, Book 2 by Karin Kallmaker writing as Laura Adams. 274 pp. Intriguing sequel to *Sleight of Hand*. ISBN 1-931513-19-8 $12.95

DRIFTING AT THE BOTTOM OF THE WORLD by Auden Bailey. 288 pp. Beautifully written first novel set in Antarctica. ISBN 1-931513-17-1 $12.95

CLOUDS OF WAR by Diana Rivers. 288 pp. Women unite to defend Zelindar!
ISBN 1-931513-12-0 $12.95

DEATHS OF JOCASTA: 2nd Micky Knight Mystery by J.M. Redmann. 408 pp. Sexy and intriguing Lambda Literary Award-nominated mystery. ISBN 1-931513-10-4 $12.95

LOVE IN THE BALANCE by Marianne K. Martin. 256 pp. The classic lesbian love story, back in print! ISBN 1-931513-08-2 $12.95

THE COMFORT OF STRANGERS by Peggy J. Herring. 272 pp. Lela's work was her passion . . . until now. ISBN 1-931513-09-0 $12.95

CHICKEN by Paula Martinac. 208 pp. Lynn finds that the only thing harder than being in a lesbian relationship is ending one. ISBN 1-931513-07-4 $11.95

TAMARACK CREEK by Jackie Calhoun. 208 pp. An intriguing story of love and danger.
ISBN 1-931513-06-6 $11.95

DEATH BY THE RIVERSIDE: 1st Micky Knight Mystery by J.M. Redmann. 320 pp. Finally back in print, the book that launched the Lambda Literary Award–winning Micky Knight mystery series. ISBN 1-931513-05-8 $11.95

EIGHTH DAY: A Cassidy James Mystery by Kate Calloway. 272 pp. In the eighth installment of the Cassidy James mystery series, Cassidy goes undercover at a camp for troubled teens. ISBN 1-931513-04-X $11.95

MIRRORS by Marianne K. Martin. 208 pp. Jean Carson and Shayna Bradley fight for a future together. ISBN 1-931513-02-3 $11.95

THE ULTIMATE EXIT STRATEGY: A Virginia Kelly Mystery by Nikki Baker. 240 pp. The long-awaited return of the wickedly observant Virginia Kelly.
ISBN 1-931513-03-1 $11.95

FOREVER AND THE NIGHT by Laura DeHart Young. 224 pp. Desire and passion ignite the frozen Arctic in this exciting sequel to the classic romantic adventure *Love on the Line*. ISBN 0-931513-00-7 $11.95

WINGED ISIS by Jean Stewart. 240 pp. The long-awaited sequel to *Warriors of Isis* and the fourth in the exciting Isis series. ISBN 1-931513-01-5 $11.95

ROOM FOR LOVE by Frankie J. Jones. 192 pp. Jo and Beth must overcome the past in order to have a future together. ISBN 0-9677753-9-6 $11.95

THE QUESTION OF SABOTAGE by Bonnie J. Morris. 144 pp. A charming, sexy tale of romance, intrigue, and coming of age. ISBN 0-9677753-8-8 $11.95

SLEIGHT OF HAND by Karin Kallmaker writing as Laura Adams. 256 pp. A journey of passion, heartbreak, and triumph that reunites two women for a final chance at their destiny. ISBN 0-9677753-7-X $11.95

MOVING TARGETS: A Helen Black Mystery by Pat Welch. 240 pp. Helen must decide if getting to the bottom of a mystery is worth hitting bottom. ISBN 0-9677753-6-1 $11.95

CALM BEFORE THE STORM by Peggy J. Herring. 208 pp. Colonel Robicheaux retires from the military and comes out of the closet. ISBN 0-9677753-1-0 $11.95

OFF SEASON by Jackie Calhoun. 208 pp. Pam threatens Jenny and Rita's fledgling relationship. ISBN 0-9677753-0-2 $11.95

WHEN EVIL CHANGES FACE: A Motor City Thriller by Therese Szymanski. 240 pp. Brett Higgins is back in another heart-pounding thriller. ISBN 0-9677753-3-7 $11.95

BOLD COAST LOVE by Diana Tremain Braund. 208 pp. Jackie Claymont fights for her reputation and the right to love the woman she chooses. ISBN 0-9677753-2-9 $11.95

THE WILD ONE by Lyn Denison. 176 pp. Rachel never expected that Quinn's wild yearnings would change her life forever. ISBN 0-9677753-4-5 $11.95

SWEET FIRE by Saxon Bennett. 224 pp. Welcome to Heroy—the town with more lesbians per capita than any other place on the planet! ISBN 0-9677753-5-3 $11.95